BUZZ AROUND THE TRACK

They Said It...

"I'm a positive person, one who doesn't rush to judge others, so my first reaction to my new client was as startling as it was unwelcome. Zack Matheson is a pain in the butt. And the best-looking man I've ever met."
—Gaby Colson

"My new PR rep says I'm a 'hottie,' which I guess is a good thing. But all I want to do is win races."
—Zack Matheson

"I need someone to take over for me when I'm on leave. I don't know if Gaby has the spine for the job. We'll see how she handles Zack, who is no one's idea of a docile client."
—Sandra Taney

"There's been bad blood between me and Zack for years, due to more than just brotherly competition. And every time I think things are getting better, something pushes us apart again."
—Trent Matheson

ABBY GAINES

Like some of her favorite NASCAR drivers, Abby Gaines's first love was open-wheel dirt track racing. But the lure of NASCAR—the speed, the power, the awesome scale—proved irresistible, just as it did for those drivers. Now Abby is thrilled to be combining her love of NASCAR with her love of writing.

The Comeback, Zack Matheson's story, is the third book Abby has written about the Matheson family, following *Back on Track* and *Checkered Past.*

When she's not writing romance novels for the Harlequin NASCAR series and for Harlequin Superromance, Abby works as editor of a speedway magazine. She lives with her husband and three children just a short drive from her favorite dirt track.

Visit Abby at www.abbygaines.com, where you'll find an extra After The End scene featuring the Mathesons, or feel free to e-mail her at abby@abbygaines.com and let her know if you enjoyed this story.

NASCAR

THE COMEBACK

Abby Gaines

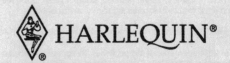

HARLEQUIN®

TORONTO • NEW YORK • LONDON
AMSTERDAM • PARIS • SYDNEY • HAMBURG
STOCKHOLM • ATHENS • TOKYO • MILAN • MADRID
PRAGUE • WARSAW • BUDAPEST • AUCKLAND

Recycling programs
for this product may
not exist in your area.

ISBN-13: 978-0-373-18531-3

THE COMEBACK

Copyright © 2010 by Harlequin Books S.A.

Abby Gaines is acknowledged as the author of this work.

NASCAR® and the NASCAR Library Collection® are registered trademarks of the National Association for Stock Car Auto Racing, Inc.

www.eHarlequin.com

Printed in U.S.A.

With love to Judith and Mark Jamieson—
with thanks for years of friendship…
and many wonderful meals!

NASCAR HIDDEN LEGACIES

The Grossos

Dean Grosso
m.
Patsy Clark Grosso

— Kent Grosso
(fiancée Tanya Wells)

— Gina Grosso
(deceased)

— Sophia Grosso
(fiancé Justin Murphy)

The Clarks

Andrew Clark
(divorced)

Patsy's brother

Garrett Clark ⑯
(Andrew's stepson)

Patsy's cousin

Jake McMasters ⑧

Kent's agent

Kane Ledger ⑦

The Claytons

Steve Clayton ⑩

— Mattie Clayton ⑭

Damon Tieri ⑪

Business partner

The Cargills

Alan Cargill (widower)

Nathan Cargill ⑤

The Branches

Maeve Branch
(div. Hilton Branch) m.
Chuck Lawrence

— Will Branch ②

— Bart Branch

— Penny Branch m.
Craig Lockhart

— Sawyer Branch

① *Scandals and Secrets*
② *Black Flag, White Lies*
③ *Checkered Past*
④ *From the Outside*
⑤ *Over the Wall*
⑥ *No Holds Barred*
⑦ *One Track Mind*
⑧ *Within Striking Distance*
⑨ *Running Wide Open*
⑩ *A Taste for Speed*
⑪ *Force of Nature*
⑫ *Banking on Hope*
⑬ *The Comeback*
⑭ *Into the Corner*
⑮ *Raising the Stakes*
⑯ *Crossing the Line*

THE FAMILIES AND THE CONNECTIONS

The Sanfords

Bobby Sanford
(deceased)
m.
Kath Sanford

— Adam Sanford ①

— Brent Sanford ⑫

— Trey Sanford ⑨

The Hunts

Dan Hunt
m.
Linda (Willard) Hunt
(deceased)

— Ethan Hunt ⑥

— Jared Hunt ⑮

— Hope Hunt ⑫

— Grace Hunt Winters ⑯
(widow of Todd Winters)

The Mathesons

Brady Matheson
(widower)
(fiancée Julie-Anne Blake)

— Chad Matheson ③

— Zack Matheson ⑬

— Trent Matheson
(fiancée Kelly Greenwood)

The Daltons

Buddy Dalton
m.
Shirley Dalton

— Mallory Dalton ④

— Tara Dalton ①

— Emma-Lee Dalton

CHAPTER ONE

GABY COLSON CONSIDERED herself a positive person, one who didn't rush to judgment of others. Which made her instinctive assessment of her new client as startling as it was unwelcome.

Zack Matheson is a pain in the butt.

Gaby tapped her pen against her chin, as she eyed Zack from across the dark lacquered desk. He'd kept her waiting three weeks—*three weeks*—for this meeting, and now that she'd finally made it into his inner sanctum at Matheson Racing's concrete-and-glass headquarters, he wouldn't talk.

And somehow, she was supposed to turn this…this chunk of granite into a media personality.

Her career in public relations, her *life,* depended on it.

Zack's gleaming gaze pinned Gaby from the other side of the desk. She was pretty sure she knew what that gleam was all about. It was anticipation that she was about to storm out of here the way his last publicist had, and leave him in peace to focus on the comeback he was planning in the NASCAR Sprint Cup Series.

Bad call, buster. Because even though her instincts shrieked that this project would be a disaster, she was desperate.

She couldn't leave until he'd agreed to the publicity program she'd devised.

Gaby stopped the nervous tapping of her pen and smiled brightly at Zack. She could tell from the way he folded his arms across his broad chest he hadn't expected that. Sandra

Taney, Gaby's boss at Motor Media Group, had said Zack wasn't the easiest guy to work with—a gross understatement—but he would eventually knuckle under and fulfill his obligations to his sponsor, Getaway Resorts. So long as Gaby was tough with him.

"No more marshmallow," Sandra had warned. They both knew Gaby's preferred style was people-pleasing and that she hadn't always picked the right people to please.

"I'm stronger than you think," Gaby had promised her boss.

Now she just had to prove it. She reminded herself that, contractually, Zack was obligated to attend this meeting. Pressing that tiny advantage, she went on. "The good news is that by anyone's standards, you're a hottie."

That wasn't flattery. She figured he already knew he was one of the best-looking men in NASCAR.

At least, he could be. If he'd smile.

Wariness settled over Zack's already guarded face, strengthening its hard planes and turning those silver-gray eyes flinty. Then for a second he seemed to relax. He didn't go so far as smiling, but the firmness in his mouth eased and Gaby wondered if the sudden glint in his eyes was humor. It vanished too soon for her to be sure.

"A hottie." He appeared to weigh the word, and though he didn't seem overjoyed by the description, at least he didn't object. "That's a good thing, right?"

"Absolutely," Gaby said eagerly, encouraged by the longest sentence he'd uttered since she'd walked in here a half hour ago. Maybe he was just slow to warm up. She could fix that. "If we're going to raise your profile in mainstream media, it helps that you take a good photo." She shrugged her acceptance of the inevitable truth.

"Does it help if I win races, too?" Zack asked.

Gaby detected irony, possibly even resentment, in the question, and decided it was wiser not to comment. Zack swiveled his padded black leather chair a half turn to gaze out through the glass wall and into the workshop, where his team was working to set up his No. 548 car for next weekend's race. The movement revealed a framed color photograph on the wall behind him—a race driver, brandishing an enormous trophy.

Gaby realized with a shock the driver was Zack. And he was smiling—no, beaming. Possibly even laughing, with a pleasure the two-dimensional confines of the photo could barely contain.

She let out a small sound of surprise, and Zack caught the direction of her gaze. "I won the NASCAR Nationwide Series five years ago," he said. "That was before—" He stopped. His gaze flickered over her, as if he was surprised he'd come close to revealing any personal details to someone like her.

No way would Gaby let him sink back into silence. Her "hottie" comment had snagged his attention—maybe she should stick with the blunt approach. She took a deep breath and said, "Before you were a has-been?"

ZACK'S MIND JERKED BACK to the woman in front of him. For the second time in as many minutes Gaby Colson had surprised him. He guessed she'd intended to shock him into participating in this discussion. Given the way she swallowed, the movement momentarily flattening her full lips, she wasn't overly comfortable with the tactic. But her direct blue gaze didn't waver.

"Is that your professional assessment of me?" he asked, grudgingly admiring her ploy.

When Sandra Taney had called to say she was assigning a new PR rep to Zack, one who would "bring him into line," Zack had pictured someone like Sandra herself—tall, forceful, liable to think she could steamroller him into taking his eye off his racing for the sake of some dumb PR campaign.

Yet nothing about the reality of Gaby matched his expectations. It wasn't just the clothes, although her mint-green sleeveless dress that molded close, but not too close, to her figure, and her low-heeled green sandals with laces that wound around a fetching pair of ankles and tied in a jaunty bow, weren't exactly kick-butt business attire.

The real surprise was that Gaby was clearly out of her depth. Once or twice during their one-sided conversation, Zack's obvious lack of enthusiasm had made her blue eyes widen and caused her to draw in a sharp breath. As if she was coming up for air one last time.

Zack couldn't figure out why Sandra had thought this new PR rep had any chance of pulling him into line, but he was grateful for one thing—Gaby would be easy to ignore.

Admittedly, he hadn't expected her "has-been" comment. But he saw that as a desperate clutch at a piece of driftwood that might save her.

He folded his arms, settled back in his chair and waited to see if she could somehow build herself a life raft. It was more fun than worrying about whether he could make a successful comeback four years after he'd quit the NASCAR Sprint Cup Series.

"You must know what the media are saying about you and your prospects," Gaby said, desperation tingeing the words. "You've had enough crashes, finished at the back in enough races, that they're saying you have no chance of a halfway decent slot on the series' points standings. I'm here to help you build a more positive image, which I believe will spill over into the press coverage of your racing."

He ignored the first part of her lecture, because although he hadn't done so well since he'd won at Daytona in February, his current poor performance was a temporary situation. One he would fix. "A more positive image sounds great," he said. "Go right ahead."

She shook her head in exasperation, and her red-gold curls bobbed around her shoulders. "I'm not a miracle worker. Your good looks will help grab the media's attention, but holding it will take more effort. I can't do it without your help."

Zack exhaled through clenched teeth. Surely she could see it was galling that his sponsor valued him for his *good looks* over his driving skills? That although he'd agreed to all kinds of public appearances for the sake of those crucial sponsorship dollars, he could never get excited about appearing in celebrity columns or lifestyle magazines.

He knew why his sponsor wanted to push him as a "sporting personality." Because they didn't believe he could win the NASCAR Sprint Cup Series. They thought getting him in a few magazines was their best chance of a return on their investment.

Maybe they were right.

"I'm aware of my contractual responsibilities to Getaway," he said. "I intend to fulfill them."

Relief washed over Gaby's face, leaving her eyes bright. "Does that mean you'll cooperate?"

"What else could it mean?" he said impatiently.

"Great." Her cheeks flushed with pleasure, and somehow that rush of color drew Zack's attention to her lips, which were full and nicely shaped, with a sheen that made him think of—

I'm losing the plot. Zack shook off all thoughts about his PR rep's mouth and focused instead on the words coming out of it. And the words were nowhere near as palatable.

"We're already behind schedule," she said. Zack took that as a dig about his making her wait three weeks for this meeting. Yeah, well, the way he'd been racing lately, his time was better spent getting himself in shape, running some practice laps. Gaby continued, "The first thing I'll do is try to interest a couple of major newspapers in featuring you in their lifestyle sections."

"Sure." Once again, he breathed easier. His life outside racing wasn't exactly exciting, he couldn't see any newspaper editor wanting to waste a reporter's time—and Zack's—pursuing such a story.

"Plus…" Her hesitation drew him back to her.

"Plus?" he prompted.

"*Now Woman* magazine is running a Bachelor of the Year

contest, centered around NASCAR drivers." She rushed the words out. "Thirty drivers from the various NASCAR national series have signed on as contestants."

"You're kidding." Zack gaped. What would induce any self-respecting guy to participate in a Bachelor of the Year contest?

"It's a great PR opportunity, especially for drivers in the series that don't get as much media coverage as the Sprint Cup." Gaby gave Zack an encouraging smile. Zack didn't smile back. "The winner will be announced at the Richmond race in September," she said.

Richmond was the last of the races that determined which twelve drivers would make the Chase for the NASCAR Sprint Cup, entitling them to contest the championship series win. They both knew Zack was unlikely to make the Chase in his current form.

He definitely wouldn't make it if he didn't put everything he had into his racing.

"No way," he said. "I'm not entering any bachelor contest."

GABY SIGHED. ONCE YOU got over the too-darned-handsome thing, there wasn't much to like about Zack Matheson.

"Are you sure? Because I'm told women find you irresistible," she said doubtfully.

Again that glint appeared in his gray eyes. "There's no accounting for taste."

"I guess you're not as sociable as some of the other drivers," she conceded reluctantly. "You're quite different from your brother."

Trent Matheson, Zack's younger brother and a former NASCAR Sprint Cup Series champion was charm-on-legs and a skilled media player. Now if *he* was her client…

"Trent just got married—he's not available for the bachelor contest, or for anything else." Zack had obviously read her thoughts. Gaby felt the seeping heat that meant her cheeks were going red again. The curse of fair skin.

"Okay, we'll forget about the bachelor contest." That wasn't marshmallow behavior, she assured herself. Zack wouldn't have had a hope of winning anyway, and the contest would have probably caused her more problems than it would have solved.

"We'll spend the next few months getting you in front of the media at every opportunity," she said. "Human interest stories—visiting kids in hospital, working with the Canine Rescue Foundation."

Like many NASCAR drivers, Zack had a couple of charitable causes he supported. It had come as no surprise to her that his favorite charity focused on dogs, not people.

"Winning races will get me lots of media attention," her client said helpfully.

Her eyes slid away from his. "Er…yes, that, too." She'd pretty much given up on the hope of Zack getting any publicity through his racing. Any *good* publicity, at least. "We need to maximize the use of your brothers in this campaign," Gaby said. "Your family is a real asset to your publicity."

Zack stiffened, but Gaby was too exhausted by the effort of holding this meeting together to wonder why. She chewed on the end of her pen. "I'll prepare new media materials to, um, reflect our new focus. We'll need photos."

"I already have photos."

"I thought we could take some of you…smiling."

"Smiling?" he said, as if she'd spoken a foreign language. "That's right."

For a long moment, his eyes held hers. Gaby didn't blink.

He leaned back in his chair. "Okay, I can do smiling." He obviously expected her to take that on trust.

"Excellent," she said. Then pushed her luck. "I want your promise you won't keep me waiting three weeks when I need to see you." Because Sandra wouldn't be convinced Gaby was on top of this job if she couldn't even talk to her client.

"That was a one-off," he said. "My contract says I have to

be available to talk to my sponsor's nominated PR representative twice a week."

This was the kind of pedantic approach to his contract that had driven Gaby's predecessor to quit. Still, he'd agreed to participate in the interviews she had planned, he'd agreed to talk to her regularly and he'd even agreed to smile.

That was more than anyone else had managed to get out of him. Gaby felt a sneaking sense of anticipation for next week's staff meeting at Motor Media Group. Sandra's doubts as to whether Gaby deserved to be on the shortlist for the promotion everyone wanted would be quashed once and for all.

Self-preservation kicked in, telling her to quit while she was ahead. She pushed her chair back. "Okay, we're about done here. I'll let you get back to work."

"We're not quite done." Zack leaned back in his seat, his hands clasped behind his head. "I understand you have a job to do, which is why I've been so cooperative."

Gaby clamped down on a dozen retorts, the most polite of which was a definition of the word *cooperative.*

"But I have a job, too," he said, "and that's to win the NASCAR Sprint Cup Series. I will meet my publicity obligations, but racing comes first."

"Okay," she said cautiously, wondering if that sounded too wimpy.

"I don't win races because I do pointless interviews or smile for the cameras," he said. "I win races when I'm one hundred percent focused on my job."

Was he about to renege on his promised *cooperation?* Panic gripped Gaby, loosened her lips. "As far as I can tell," she said, "you don't win races at all."

His head jerked back.

"You do know, don't you, that Getaway has threatened to pull its sponsorship before the season is up if they don't see a better return on their money?" She continued, taking advantage of his stunned silence. "I don't care what you do when you're on the track, but when you make an appearance for your sponsor, whether the media are present or not, I want one hundred percent of your concentration."

No marshmallow would have said that, she thought with satisfaction.

He stood, a movement that managed to be both graceful and intimidating. He was just shy of six feet tall, and his loose-fitting polo shirt couldn't hide his lean strength. He ran a hand through his thick, dark hair, which she now realized had a wave in it, one that wasn't visible in his photos.

"How exactly did you get to be the boss of me?" he demanded, looming so close that she could see a tiny scar at the corner of his mouth.

Gaby caught the clean, fresh smell of soap and mint and man. She gulped, trying to corral her thoughts in the face of sensory overload. "Everyone else chickened out."

Zack stared at her. Then he laughed.

Darn, she wished he hadn't done that, despite what she'd said about wanting him to smile. Turned out laughter lightened his eyes and opened his face so he looked almost boyish. And even more devastatingly handsome. Her knees turned to water—she couldn't have stood if she'd tried.

He grinned, and she had the mortifying thought that he knew exactly the effect he was having on her.

"Okay, Gaby." Had he said her name before? She thought not, because hearing those two familiar syllables spoken in his deep voice sent a little shiver through her. "You obviously have a bee in your bonnet about this publicity stuff."

A *bee?* It was her job, for Pete's sake.

"I like a quiet life," he said, "which means I need you off my back. In the interests of my own sanity, I'm going to agree that when I'm on the publicity trail, I'll be all yours. One hundred percent. Deal?"

"Uh…deal," she said, looking for the catch.

"Now—" he glanced at his watch, dismissing her "—why

don't you go find a reporter who wants to write about my preference for butter over margarine, and I'll get back to preparing for my next race."

This time, his smile was cherubic. Gaby felt like Pandora, right after she let a load of unimagined troubles out of the box.

CHAPTER TWO

THE CHICAGO TRACK wasn't as crowded on Thursday, qualifying day, as it would be for Saturday's race, but still the atmosphere gave Gaby a buzz. The noise level had been steadily building over the past couple of hours, and with the late afternoon sunshine reflecting off the gleaming, multicolored lineup of race team haulers in the garage area, it was hard to worry. She loved this sport—she loved her job.

And she had just the right publicity strategy for Zack this weekend. It wouldn't matter if Zack made a mess of the great interview she'd scheduled, because it involved his family, as well. Every other Matheson had a gift for dealing with the media, even Zack's gruff father, Brady.

Gaby flashed the hard-card that told the security guard at the entrance to the garage area that she was attached to Matheson Racing, and headed into organized chaos. Today was almost as stressful as race day—if a driver qualified among the front-runners for the race, he'd have a much easier job when the green flag fell on Saturday.

Zack's qualifying this season had been "patchy," as one NASCAR correspondent had described it in a major newspaper earlier this week. But he'd qualified in twelfth position today. Gaby imagined that had been a relief. Having to work his way up past a couple of dozen of the world's top race drivers was a daunting prospect for anyone, let alone a driver trying to make a comeback.

Fleetingly, she wondered why Zack was so set on this

comeback, when by all accounts his race track simulation software business in Atlanta was a big success. It must be torture, returning to a sport where he'd been one of the brightest stars, only to find his light had faded.

Gaby reached Zack's garage area. He was ranked twenty-second in points for the season to date, which meant his car and hauler were some distance from the pits. Zack's brother Trent, sitting fifth, enjoyed a more convenient location.

Gaby found Zack deep in conversation with his older brother and team owner, Chad Matheson, in the office at the front of the hauler. Chad glanced up as she entered.

"Excuse me, I'm sorry…am I interrupting?" Gaby could have kicked herself for her hesitancy. When she'd first volunteered to work with Zack, she and Sandra had met with Chad to explain the change in personnel. Chad had been unconvinced Gaby could handle his brother.

She tried again, with a brisker, "Zack, I'm glad I found you."

He raised an eyebrow. "I do tend to be at the track on race weekends."

Gaby ignored that inanity. "I need to brief you about an interview I've arranged with the local Chicago newspaper."

"I'm busy," Zack said, "planning my race."

Chad sat back from the built-in table, arms folded across his chest, interest evident in the alert lines of his body.

"The reporter—" too high and squeaky, Gaby cleared her throat "—wants to talk about the challenges inherent in making a comeback."

"Is it that guy Pete Jameson?" Zack perked up. The newspaper's NASCAR commentator was highly respected in racing circles.

It broke Gaby's heart to answer the question. "It's not Pete. This guy is more of a…uh…actually, he's the advice columnist."

"A *shrink?*" Zack said, outraged.

"He's writing a feature, a *major* feature that might even end up the lead in the Saturday sports section, on athletes overcoming past problems." She saw the beginnings of a pleased smile on Chad's face. "The reporter would also like to interview one of your brothers," she said. "Chad, maybe you could do it."

Silence.

"I'd be happy to," Chad said, so neutrally she knew he didn't mean it.

Didn't Chad want to help his brother? Now Zack had his arms folded, too, mirroring Chad. The two men eyed each other, Zack's expression challenging, Chad's frustrated.

Gaby had no idea what was going on between them, but her hope that Chad would salvage the interview if Zack botched it quickly faded. She groaned inwardly.

"Gaby, how do you think Zack will do in this weekend's race?" Chad's tone was casual, but his gaze was sharp.

Truthfully? She imagined it would go the way every race had recently. Zack would struggle to hold on to his starting position, and would gradually slip down to finish somewhere in the twenties.

Zack's smoky gray eyes met hers. He was challenging her the way he'd challenged his brother a moment ago.

To do what?

My job, she thought. Her job was to represent Zack to the public, and right now the public included his brother.

"I think Zack's strong qualifying will boost his confidence," she said. "Don't be surprised if you see him near the front of the field."

Chad didn't look surprised...he looked astounded.

So did Zack. He didn't smile at Gaby—he'd probably used up his entire season's allocations of smiles at their last meeting—but he nodded slowly. His gray eyes were so intense that she felt almost as if he'd reached out and touched her. Her breath shortened.

Before Chad could reply, the office door opened. His wife, Brianna, walked in. Gaby seized the chance to break the connection with Zack and greeted Brianna with a smile.

"Hi, darling." Chad's face lit up as he stood. Anyone would think he hadn't seen his wife in weeks, when in fact Gaby had spotted the couple lunching together a couple of hours ago.

Brianna kissed him on the mouth. Brief though the kiss was, she was positively starry-eyed when she turned to the others. Gaby felt awkward witnessing that kiss right after she'd....*what?* Traded *looks* with Zack?

"Hi, Gaby. Zack, nice qualifying." Brianna smiled at her brother-in-law, and Gaby was surprised to see one side of Zack's mouth quirk and his face soften. On the heels of her surprise, Gaby felt something alarmingly like envy—envy that Brianna was the recipient of that mellowing.

"Chad, honey," Brianna continued, "the Energy Oil guys would like to chat when you have a moment." She'd recently taken over as team liaison for Trent's sponsors, of which Energy Oil was the biggest. Her late father had been the founder of Getaway Resorts, and it was Brianna who'd recommended the company sponsor Zack. But after her dad's death and her reunion with Chad, from whom she'd separated right after their Vegas wedding, the cousin who'd taken over at Getaway had been uncomfortable about a conflict of interest. So Brianna now contributed her considerable marketing skills to Trent's team.

"Sure, let's go." Chad laced his fingers through Brianna's. As they reached the doorway, he turned back to Gaby. "Don't be surprised—" he nodded an acknowledgment that he was borrowing her words "—if you're wrong about the race."

He and Brianna left. Gaby stared at the door Chad had closed behind him. "Did I hear right?" she demanded. "Did your brother just tell me not to be surprised if you screw up on Saturday?"

No answer from Zack. She turned and found his face shuttered. No sign of that connection that she must have imagined between them.

"Yeah," he said, expressionless.

"Why would he do that?" she asked, still rattled by that momentary, inexplicable envy of Brianna.

"Chad and I don't always get along."

His shrug said it was no big deal, but Gaby discerned pain in his eyes. "What about you and Trent?" Maybe the reporter could get the family perspective from Zack's younger brother.

"Trent and I definitely don't get along."

Great. Still, some rivalry between brothers was inevitable when they were both after the same thing. "Your father, maybe?"

Zack shifted in his seat. "Dad has a lot on his mind. Julie-Anne's daughter is about to arrive back in town." Brady Matheson had eloped with his secretary Julie-Anne earlier in the year; industry gossip suggested the woman's daughter, an adventure tour guide in Asia, disapproved. "He won't want to be bothered about some shrink article," Zack said firmly.

If Zack had a healthy relationship with his father, Brady would drop everything to help his son.

"What you're saying is, you don't get along with anyone," Gaby said.

His eyes narrowed. "I get along fine with my sisters-in-law. And with Julie-Anne. Now, if you've finished analyzing my relationships, maybe I could get back to my race prep."

"We need to talk more about this interview."

"If you write up a briefing, I promise I'll say whatever you tell me." He crossed to the door, held it open.

From the set of his jaw Gaby could tell she wouldn't get any further with him now.

Pesky NASCAR driver.

As she passed him, only just managing not to flounce, Zack caught hold of her arm. A band of heat formed where his fingers curved around her flesh, locking her in place, triggering a tightening throughout her body. *What the heck?*

"By the way," he said, "thanks for telling Chad you think I'll be up front in the race."

"I—it's called spin," she stammered. "I was doing my job."

His hand fell away; Gaby fought the urge to rub her arm. "So you don't believe it?" He sounded annoyed.

Not half as annoyed as she was about his lack of enthusiasm for her interview, and his inability to get on well enough with his family that one of them might support him in the media. And about her own reaction to him just now. Deliberately, she didn't answer his question. "You'll have that briefing by eight tonight."

His growl of dissatisfaction almost lifted her spirits. Almost, but not quite.

WHEN THE GREEN FLAG dropped on Saturday, Zack made two early passes that had his crew chief, Dave Harmon, smiling through his habitual dourness.

"Zack's on fire today," Chad commented to Gaby, who was watching the screen at the base of the war wagon with him.

"He looks amazing," she said honestly. The cars were on lap forty, about to pit for the first time, and she'd never seen Zack with such control over his car, such mastery of the track.

The pit stop was fast and smooth, and Dave gave the team a thumbs-up as Zack headed out after just thirteen seconds. As the laps went by, he began to pass cars, until he was running fifth. Then he passed Trent.

"Fourth," Gaby breathed, amazed that her own prediction had come true. "Do you think…"

Chad hushed her with a glance. "We've been here before." The implication was *And then it's all gone south.* Gaby tried to calm her mounting excitement. But she couldn't help thinking ahead to today's interview. If Zack finished fourth or better, the paper's motorsport reporter would want to talk to him.

Sandra Taney would be thrilled, and so would Getaway Resorts. Gaby pulled out her notebook, began jotting down some possible angles for Zack to address. Whether he would listen to her advice or not was another matter, but…

A roar rose from the crowd—horror, not excitement. Gaby

refocused on the screen, became aware of Chad cursing along-side her. Then she saw it. The electric blue No. 548 car—Zack's car—had hit the wall. The crumpled mess slid to a halt, cars swerving around it. As she watched, heart in her mouth, Zack's window-net came down, and his arm emerged in a wave, a sign that he was okay. But his race was over.

"Looks like you'll have plenty of media interest in Zack's performance," Chad said ironically.

Gaby's heart was still thudding from the shock of seeing Zack's battered car. "It might help if you had some sympathy for him," she said sharply. Good grief, what was wrong with her? She pressed her fingers to her lips, silencing any other rogue criticisms of Zack's team boss.

But Chad's glance was pitying, rather than angry. "After Zack's let you down a hundred times, you might have less sympathy for him yourself," he said.

"Not every crash is avoidable."

"That one was." Chad eyed the monitor, where Zack was now standing on the infield. "Zack's head isn't in the right place to run well this season, and nothing I do can get it there."

Gaby wondered how hard he had tried. *None of my business,* she told herself. *My job is to put a good spin on this for the reporters.* Thinking aloud, she said, "I'll emphasize how strong Zack's performance was right up until the crash, how it's a sign of good things to come."

Chad sighed. "Good luck with that." He climbed the ladder to the top of the war wagon, where Zack's crew chief had pulled off his headphones in disgust.

Gaby half jogged to the infield care center, where she knew Zack would have been taken. True to Chad's prediction, several reporters wanted a heads-up on the crash that had sent her client from fourth place to oblivion. She promised Zack would be available to answer questions as soon as the medics released him.

Inside, she found Zack sitting on the edge of a hospital-style bed, his wrist in a sling.

"Just a precaution," the doctor explained when she saw Gaby's alarm. "There's a little swelling but the X-ray didn't show any bones broken."

"I'm fine." Zack scowled. He looked like a very bad-tempered angel.

"Then take that sling off," Gaby ordered. The photographers would pounce on the opportunity to snap an injured Zack.

"Good idea," he said, ignoring the doctor's tutting.

Turned out that was where his compliance peaked. Outside, Zack dodged most of the reporters' questions, and offered monosyllabic replies to those he deigned to answer. When the advice columnist from the Chicago newspaper appeared for his interview with Zack, Gaby had a sinking feeling things would only get worse.

They adjourned to the media center where, to his credit, Zack's first answers were right in line with Gaby's briefing. But then the journalist asked, "To what extent are your difficulties on the track symptomatic of problems within your family?"

"None of your damn business," Zack growled.

The guy beamed and ignored Gaby's attempts to move the conversation into smoother waters. So did Zack. Obviously still smarting from his race, and maybe from Chad's lack of support earlier, he let fly several colorful comments—none of them positive—about family loyalty, racing and the futility of psychologists trying to analyze this stuff.

Did he have a sponsorship death wish?

After the interview, Zack headed for his motor home. Gaby followed, her anger propelling her forward at a pace that matched the stride of his much longer legs.

He glanced sideways. "What are you puffing so hard about? I admit that interview didn't go according to plan, but like you said, the guy's writing a feature about sports in general. Anything I said will only be a small part."

"You think because he's an agony uncle he can't, and

won't, write a news story when a juicy one lands in his lap?" she demanded.

His pace slowed momentarily. "I didn't give him anything newsworthy."

"'Comeback Zack' blows his stack," Gaby said in a headline voice.

He pffed. "I had a great race today, right up until the crash. Any balanced reporting will—"

"Any balanced reporting will look at your last ten finishes and see four crashes," she railed.

His jaw tightened. "I also had two top-tens—you're paid to make sure those get covered, too. I'm paid to drive the car."

"At least I'm doing my best to earn my salary," she muttered. "Which, by the way, doesn't cover me for achieving the impossible."

Next week's meeting with Sandra, the one she'd been looking forward to, loomed in her head. So much for her plan to show off the positive coverage she was achieving for Zack.

CHAPTER THREE

WHEN GABY'S SHOULDERS sagged, Zack had the oddest urge to pull her close, to comfort her.

It was guilt, he told himself. Guilt about messing up that interview. It wasn't Gaby's fault he'd raced like a rookie, nor that the journalist had asked such intrusive questions.

Actually, it *was* her fault about the questions, she should have known better than to set him up to talk about that stuff.

Still, he didn't like to see the droop of her mouth, and the furrow in her brow that suggested she was working hard to keep her equilibrium.

He knew how she felt. He'd really thought he might make a top-five finish today. To have the race end the way so many others had...

"I'll call Getaway, prepare them for more bad press," she said. "Then I'll get to work on setting up your next media appearance. For which we'll spend a lot more time preparing."

The urge to touch her vanished. Zack shoved his hands in his pockets. "I need to spend a lot more time preparing for my next race."

Whatever sympathy he'd imagined she might have had for him before the race was gone. She gave a little hiss. "You promised to cooperate."

They'd reached the motor home lot. Zack decided to end this conversation now. He stopped at the gate and indicated to the security guard that Gaby wasn't coming in.

"I will cooperate." He ignored the angry quiver of her chin and said calmly, "Whenever I can."

He slipped past the security guard and lifted his hand in farewell. Gaby glared at him, obviously not wanting to fight in front of the guard. Fine by him. Zack had to do his job, and if that meant she couldn't do hers, that was too bad. He walked away without looking back.

SANDRA TANEY'S HAND RESTED on her swollen belly, and she smiled.

"Junior kicking again?" Gaby handed her boss a soda from the well-stocked fridge on the Taney Motorsports airplane, and sat down opposite her. Next to Gaby, her colleague Kylie Treadway sipped a cola. Anita Latimer and Leah Gibbs, the other Motor Media Group representatives flying to the track in Indianapolis this weekend, were sticking with water.

"Never stops," Sandra said proudly. "I've warned Gideon his son is going to play pro football, not basketball."

As Gaby refastened her seat belt she laughed, as much out of relief as out of amusement—any delay to the inevitable discussion of her client situation was welcome.

"I'm sure Taney can handle it." Gaby popped the top on her soda can. Sandra's husband Gideon Taney, owner of Taney Motorsports, had been a talented basketball player in his youth, but he'd chosen to start his own sporting goods business rather than turn pro.

Sandra's smile turned dreamy as she craned to see her husband, who was watching a recording of the last race at Indianapolis in the TV area at the back of the plane. "He can handle anything."

For a woman with a reputation as one of the hardest-hitting PR operatives in NASCAR, Sandra was a pile of mush when it came to her husband. And six-foot-four Taney, as everyone but Sandra called him, had it just as bad for his wife. Gaby had never seen a couple who adored each other so much.

She'd assumed two such strong-willed individuals would clash beyond survival. But while Sandra and Taney had "discussions" that bordered on explosive, their love always shone through. They seemed to thrive on the sparks.

That's what I want. A man who would respect Gaby's goals and desires the way Taney respected Sandra's. She would never again let a man convince her that love meant sacrificing her goals for his.

"Let's get down to business," Sandra said, all dreaminess evaporating. Her gaze scanned the group, resting longer on Gaby than it did on the other women.

Uh-oh.

"I'm sorry we had to wait this long for our staff meeting," Sandra continued, "but Will's supposed health scare has kept me flat out." Earlier this week, medical tests suggesting that Will Branch, Taney Motorsports' NASCAR Sprint Cup Series driver, had mononucleosis—which would demand a break from racing—had been leaked by a clinic administrator. Gaby guessed Sandra couldn't have slept much the past few days, in her quest for the source of the leak and the evidence needed to prove to the world that the mono test was someone else's, and Will was perfectly healthy.

"You did an incredible job, Sandra," Kylie said. Kylie had been Will's rep until Sandra and Taney had realized they could spend more time together if Sandra represented Will.

Gaby wished she'd been first with the compliment. Not that Sandra liked people kissing up—but she definitely liked people showing leadership.

Especially now, when she was looking for someone to run Motor Media Group after she had her baby. She would still attend races as Taney's wife, and knowing Sandra she wouldn't be able to resist phoning in to the company she'd founded. But the day-to-day operations would be in the hands of someone at the office.

Gaby planned to be that someone.

So did Kylie and Anita.

Sandra had made her reservations about Gaby clear when she'd agreed to consider her for the job along with her peers. Volunteering to rep Zack had been the best way for Gaby to prove her account management skills.

Gaby swallowed hard and wondered if there was any chance her boss hadn't seen the headlines this week.

"Anita, let's start with you," Sandra said.

Anita talked through the work she was doing for Bart Branch, Will's twin brother and "her" driver. She'd achieved some excellent press coverage this week. She'd also managed to interest a NASCAR Nationwide Series team in hiring Motor Media Group.

"Great job, I'm seriously impressed." Sandra liked winning new business. She also believed in giving credit where it was due, one reason why working for her was so rewarding. "Kylie?"

Kylie managed Danny Cruise. They all knew Danny could be reticent with the press, which made Kylie's eight-page profile in a lifestyle magazine even more special. Sandra nodded her approval.

"Gaby," she said, her voice noticeably cooler.

Gaby darted a quick glance out the window. They were flying over farmland—serene, beautiful…and way too high to bail out of this conversation. "Not the best week in Zack Matheson's career." She tried to sound calm and in control, even though she couldn't have had a worse grip on Zack if he'd been a shadow.

"The understanding you told me you and your client came to at your first meeting…" Sandra opened her briefcase and pulled out the sports section of the Chicago paper. The reporter had done exactly what Gaby feared, and written a hard-hitting news story. Sandra tapped the headline with an accusing finger. "Was it an understanding that he can walk all over you?"

There was no amusement in her tone. Sandra had a great sense of humor, but she took her work seriously.

Gaby stiffened. "Of course not. I briefed Zack on the postrace interviews, but he chose to go his own way."

"Then you didn't do a good enough job," Sandra said. The downside of her being so quick to praise her staff was that she got tough equally fast, and she didn't necessarily wait for a private moment. "I appointed you to manage Zack because you assured me you could keep him in line."

And because no one else wanted the job. Gaby knew better than to try to deflect the criticism. Aware of Kylie's and Anita's sympathetic glances, she said, "Zack's not an easy client, Sandra—you've lost two account managers thanks to his acting out, and two others only stayed at the company on the basis they wouldn't have to work with him. Did you expect me to have a handle on him after only a few days?"

Sandra looked surprised to be challenged. "Perhaps not," she conceded. "But I'd expect to see some of your influence in this article. Instead, I see a driver with a chip on his shoulder and no self-restraint." She leaned back and rubbed her abdomen, as if the baby was kicking in protest at the bad job Gaby had done. "Rob Hudson at Getaway phoned me to express his disappointment."

If Gaby hadn't known how serious it was to have a sponsor complain about her, Kylie's indrawn breath would have filled her in.

The plane lurched, buffeted by a sudden gust of wind, and nausea churned in Gaby's stomach. "You know I did a good job for Trey Sanford." Her previous client had been a dream to work with. Complications in his personal life had kept her on her toes, but Trey's sound media instincts had made them an effective team.

"You did, which gives me some hope. But I'd like to hear your plans for doing things differently with Zack," Sandra said. "So would Rob."

"As a driver, Zack has moments of sheer genius, but they're outweighed by moments of impulsiveness," Gaby began.

Watching the footage of the past few races, she'd been mystified by Zack's habit of suddenly blowing a strong position. It didn't fit with the coolly controlled man she knew. "If he could cut back the impulses and play up the genius…" She trailed off. The best PR plan in the world wouldn't help him do that. "I believe he's the same off the track," she continued. "We need to harness the genius, get rid of the impulse, in his media appearances."

"No easy task." Sandra didn't sound quite as mad as she had a few minutes earlier. Gaby breathed a little easier.

"Have you thought about putting him in the Bachelor of the Year contest?" Sandra asked. "Bart's getting a lot of publicity out of that."

"I suggested the contest, but he won't do it." Gaby realized her error as her boss frowned. "Even if he would, I couldn't trust him not to do more harm than good to his reputation." Great, why didn't she just shoot herself in both feet?

"What I'm hearing," Sandra said, "is you're not strong enough to convince Zack of what's in his best interest."

Kylie and Anita traded knowing glances, glances that said, *She won't get the top job.*

Everyone in the company knew Gaby had turned down a promotion last year under pressure from her fiancé at the time. This time around, she'd been running from behind from the start.

"Ladies," Sandra said, addressing Gaby's colleagues, "why don't you join Taney for a while?"

There was a flurry of activity while the other women gathered up their bags and drinks and headed to the TV nook. Taney looked surprised to see them; then he directed an understanding look at his wife.

Gaby, alone now with her boss, tugged her seat belt tighter.

"Gaby…" Sandra's hesitation was uncharacteristic. "Are you seeing anyone at the moment?"

"Seeing…you mean *dating?*" Gaby stared at her.

"It's just, you told me you would do what it took to get this promotion," Sandra said. "You're not delivering, which isn't like you. I wondered if maybe you're…distracted."

"Even if I was seeing someone, which I'm not, I wouldn't let that happen again," Gaby said. "My job is my number one priority, and I've learned my lesson about letting a man get in the way of that."

Sandra nodded.

"Zack Matheson will do what we need him to do," Gaby promised. "I'll stake my reputation on it."

"You already did," Sandra said.

Something cold and serious in her blue eyes hollowed Gaby's stomach. "One bad article won't affect your decision about who takes over during your maternity leave, will it?" she blurted.

"It's not one bad article, Gaby." Sandra leaned forward as best as her bulk would allow. "I agreed to consider you for the position because your administrative background gives you an excellent understanding of the business, and because you assured me you've moved on from the attitude that had you turning down that promotion last year. But I made it clear I'll appoint someone who can run the firm the way I do. That means someone who puts the company first and doesn't take garbage from people."

"I don't—"

"I need someone who'll fight for my business," Sandra said. "You're not that person. I'm taking you off the shortlist."

Gaby's lungs constricted; she couldn't breathe. "No!" The word came out a squeak, using up the last of her air. She cupped her hands over her mouth and nose, and finally found breath.

Sandra eyed her in alarm. Gaby dropped her hands, fought for composure.

This promotion was her big chance to secure her future, to ease her cash-strapped elderly parents' worries, and her own, about how she would be provided for. With her lack of a college education and her overly administrative background, no other company would even consider her for this kind of job.

She needed to rescue this situation, right now.

"What if I get Zack into the Bachelor of the Year contest?" she asked.

"You just said he won't do it."

"That was marshmallow-me talking." Gaby attempted a small joke. "Sandra, I admit, I'm on a learning curve with Zack, but I'll learn faster, I'll make it happen."

"You really think you can persuade him into the contest?" Sandra asked, patently unconvinced.

"I have to," Gaby said. A subtle shift in the engine noise told her the aircraft had begun its descent. She didn't want Sandra to get off this plane with the last thought on her mind being that Gaby was a no-go. Any savvy PR operative knew that last impressions were almost as important as first impressions. "And if he does—if Zack enters the contest and makes a real effort, if we can honestly say Getaway is delighted— will you put me back on the shortlist?"

"I'd need to see quite a transformation," Sandra said honestly. "In Zack, and in yourself."

"You'll see it," Gaby promised. "Can I get back on the shortlist?"

Sandra glanced at Taney and the other women, then back at Gaby. "I'll keep an open mind."

"Thanks, Sandra, you won't regret it."

Gaby was certain of that. The prospect of her prickly client being a contender for Bachelor of the Year was mind-boggling, but she would make it happen.

CHAPTER FOUR

ZACK HAD RACED BETTER in Indianapolis—he'd finished eleventh, a result he attributed to the fact he'd spent more time in the gym than usual and less time on his public image. Fortunately, his sponsor didn't hear that.

When Gaby had called him to confirm their Tuesday morning meeting, he told her he'd realized his physical fitness wasn't up to race-winning level. He'd asked his trainer to devise a tough new program.

"You're okay to meet in the gym, right?" he asked.

"Of course," she said. After all, he needed to be in peak physical condition for the bachelor contest.

Now, she sat on a weight bench in the Matheson Racing gym, waiting for Zack to move to a piece of equipment that involved less exertion than the rowing machine, so she could broach the bachelor contest without raising her voice. She couldn't help noticing that Zack was already in fantastic condition. Not overbulked, his tank top revealed just the right amount of lean muscle in those strong arms and broad, perfectly proportioned shoulders. The rowing machine showed off his long legs and powerful chest.

Through the mirror that ran along the end wall of the gym, Zack caught her looking. His eyebrows quirked. Gaby tore her gaze away and focused on the blank page of her notebook. She'd all but lost her chance at the promotion, and here she was admiring her client's body.

It was his mind she needed to focus on…and that was

every bit as intriguing. He was smart—as she'd told Sandra, sometimes he was a genius. And yet he kept screwing up, and he was more vulnerable than he should be to the ebb and flow of family dynamics. Gaby sighed.

"What's the problem?" Zack asked.

She jumped—it was the most he'd said since she'd arrived—and closed the notebook. "Just thinking about the next step in our campaign."

"Do you ever stop thinking about your work?" he asked.

"Do you ever stop thinking about yours?"

He frowned, "No, but…"

Gaby's eyes narrowed. "But yours is more important than mine?"

"I didn't say that."

"Mine's more challenging than yours," she said with grim certainty.

He snorted and Gaby realized she enjoyed talking so bluntly to him.

Zack adjusted the settings on the rowing machine to a higher level. "So what did you come up with?" It didn't seem fair he could still talk while hauling that much weight.

Gaby took a deep breath. Since he'd asked her outright, she would just say it. She raised her voice over the whir of the machine. "That your best chance of satisfying your sponsor is the Bachelor of the Year contest."

"NO WAY." ZACK'S RHYTHM faltered; he scowled at Gaby. "I told you, I'm not doing that contest."

"Thanks for giving it your serious consideration," she said, her normally full lips tight. The light in her eyes faded, then something flickered there that might have been hurt. Or panic. Then again, it might have been the intent to whack him over the head with a barbell.

"It's nothing personal, Gaby." Dammit, why was he defending his perfectly reasonable response? "You're my fifth

MMG account manager since January." He saw her gathering steam and added quickly, "I'm not proud of that statistic. But it's a sign that I'm just not good at PR."

Gaby's chin lifted; by now he knew that meant she was getting ready to argue. "No one's asking you to be someone you're not," she said. "You're not a guy who'll churn out happy sound-bites for the media, and that's fine. We need to harness your natural style to make the best impression."

That would have made sense, if she hadn't been talking about the bachelor contest. Zack eyed Gaby. In her cream-colored wrap dress, she looked as cool and delectable as vanilla ice cream. It was weird—she got prettier every time he saw her.

Zack stopped rowing, ignoring the beeped protest of the electronic timer and grabbed his towel. He rubbed down his face, shoulders and back. He'd reached his chest by the time he became aware Gaby was sneaking surreptitious glances at him. Hmm, Ms. Vanilla Ice cream wasn't as cool as she appeared....

He tamped down the awareness. "I don't feel right about this whole PR business," he said. "What's the point of having a great image, if the reality doesn't live up to it? It's better to put my effort into fixing reality."

"You mean, you intend to work on your personality defects?"

He stretched his arms behind his head, saw the reluctant way her gaze followed the movement. "I intend to work on my racing."

She lost interest in his physique, snapped her eyes back to his.

"I'm sorry," he said, and he almost meant it, because Gaby had tried hard, and he had to admit, he liked her. "But the contest isn't going to happen."

Gaby blinked rapidly. Hell, was she going to cry? Zack put out a hand toward her, then pulled it back. Just because she looked touchable, didn't mean he got to touch her.

She sucked in her cheeks as if that might help keep the

floodgates closed, and it had the effect of pursing her lips. She looked odd. But somehow cute. And vulnerable. He winced. "Can't you just quit the account, like all the others?" he asked. "Make this somebody else's problem."

She shook her head vigorously, too upset to speak. For Pete's sake, it was only a stupid bachelor contest.

"If you're worried about how it looks," Zack said, "I'll tell Sandra you were the best rep I ever had." Dammit, she looked even closer to tears. One of his previous account managers had been a frequent crier, and Zack had never felt one iota of the guilt that was rending him now. "I'll tell Getaway, too," he promised. "It's the truth, you know. No one else has got me to listen to them the way you have."

Gaby's response was to squeeze her eyes closed and say nothing. Zack was debating whether he should sneak out and let her cry in peace, when Trent came into the gym.

"Hi, Trent," Zack said loudly, figuring he should alert Gaby to his brother's presence. She stiffened, then slowly opened her eyes and released the tension in her face.

"Howdy." Trent darted a curious glance at Gaby. "Hey, Gaby."

"Trent, how are you?" She sounded her normal self, to Zack's relief.

"Couldn't be better, what with winning at Indianapolis and all." Trent gave Gaby the dazzling smile he couldn't seem to hold back, even now that he was married. Zack knew, as everyone else did, that Trent was nuts about Kelly, his wife, who was the team's sports psychologist. He'd never so much as look at another woman, but that damned smile sure had women looking at him.

"You had a great race," Gaby agreed.

It dawned on Zack that she was unmoved by his brother's charm. Probably because she was so stressed—her fingers were curled over the edge of the weight bench in a white-knuckled grip. Zack wasn't about to quibble over the reason for her lack of interest in Trent. His brother had won enough this week, this year, the past few years, without scoring Zack's PR account manager, too.

She's not mine. Hadn't he just suggested she quit?

"I hope you're giving this guy some lessons in how to boost his image," Trent said to Gaby. "After last week's headlines, it'll take a miracle."

Typical Trent—when he saw a pot of trouble, he just had to stir it. Against his better judgment, Zack tensed. Although the words had changed since they were kids, Trent had always known how to wind him up. He did it out of kid-brother instinct rather than malice, but when you were as hung up as Zack knew he was…

Gaby's eyes had narrowed to slits. "I'm the first to agree Zack doesn't have your obvious media appeal."

Given the conversation they'd just had, Zack figured he deserved that.

"And he can be a pain in the butt," Gaby said pointedly.

Trent chuckled.

Zack felt his face tighten. Okay, okay, he'd been a jerk. She didn't need to abandon his side so completely, did she?

Why wouldn't she? Dammit, maybe he shouldn't have rushed into telling her to quit. Now, he felt oddly bereft.

"That's why from here on out we plan to emphasize Zack's hidden depths," she said.

Zack started; Trent's smile disappeared. "Zack has hidden depths?"

"I don't expect everyone to be able to see them," she said kindly. "Zack is…the thinking woman's NASCAR driver."

Trent gaped, then as the implication sank in, colored up in a way Zack had never been able to make him.

Suddenly enjoying himself, Zack said, "Gaby, I'm sure you intend no disrespect to Trent's wife."

"None at all," Gaby agreed. "Hidden depths, while undeniably attractive, can be difficult to live with." Huh, another dig at him. Zack found himself grinning. "Not everyone wants that," she said acidly.

Zack thought about all the PR operatives who'd quit his campaign the last eight months. "But you don't give up that easily."

In that moment, he knew for sure she wasn't about to quit. His heart thudded with the same relief he felt when he passed a car out on the track. Only this felt better. An unfamiliar stretching sensation in his cheeks told him he was grinning wider than he had in a long time.

"You guessed it," she said. "I'm absolutely committed to you."

The room turned stifling. Zack drew in a slow, measured breath.

"We're still talking about PR, right?" Trent asked. He was better than most men at picking up on subtleties.

"Of course," Gaby said, her eyes on Zack.

Trent yawned theatrically. "If you have the patience to find my brother's hidden depths, you'll earn every penny his desperate sponsor is paying you." By Trent's standards, it was an ineffective shot. He glanced around the gym, and smirked. "Don't know why I'm here, I'm fit enough already."

With a wink at Gaby, he slung his towel over his shoulder and left. Despite the wink, despite the familiar swagger, it was a retreat.

Gaby had run Trent out of town.

A curious warmth spread through Zack, starting in his chest, then filling every inch of him. He watched her flexing her fingers, which must now be aching from gripping that seat. She was staring after Trent, as women often did, but she looked more irritated than excited.

"Did you mean what you said?" Zack asked. "About me having hidden depths?" Because last time she'd said something nice about him, to Chad, she'd admitted it was just *spin*. That still stung.

She turned wide blue eyes to him, and nodded. "I also meant it about you being a pain in the butt."

He'd didn't doubt that. "You defended me," he said slowly. Not that he needed defending, of course. He'd been looking out for his own interests longer than he could remember. But still...

"Trent was being a jerk," Gaby said. "Even more than you were."

That damned warmth was fuzzing Zack's brain; he struggled to get a grip on his thoughts. He took a step toward her, not sure what he was looking for, but somehow certain she had it.

"You're not easy to deal with, Zack." Her words came out so quiet, he strained to hear. "But I do think you have some amazing abilities."

"Uh..." No one whose opinion he valued had said anything like that to him in years; Zack wasn't sure how to reply. "Thanks." Not exactly original, but heartfelt.

She clasped her hands in her lap. Her fingers were slim, her nails gleaming with a pale polish.

"Did you mean what you said?" she asked. "About me being the best PR rep you've had?"

"Absolutely." He nodded for emphasis.

She shoved a curl behind her ear. It sprang right out again, and Zack found himself moving instinctively to fix it. His fingers tangled with hers, next to her face.

Gaby froze. Zack registered the brush of that silky lock of hair, the warmth of her fingers. Her breath came faster, but she didn't remove her fingers from his.

He wanted to pull her to her feet, to fasten his mouth to hers, to explore...

Bad idea, Zack told himself. *Don't get carried away, just because she said something nice.* Women said nice things to him all the time.

Yeah, but not like that.

He let go of her hand, and Gaby looked down at it as if she could still feel the same current that coursed through him.

"I can't do the bachelor contest," he said abruptly. "But if you can convince one of those women's magazines to interview me, I'll spend as long you like preparing for it, and I'll say exactly what you want."

She blinked, stared at him, then visibly regrouped. "Really?"

He gritted his teeth. "I'll even take my shirt off for a photo."

Her hiccup sounded suspiciously like a giggle. "That probably won't be necessary."

He blew out a breath of relief. "I'd do it, though," he assured her.

She looked so happy, she might start skipping around the gym. But she said calmly, "Thank you, Zack."

He grunted, already wishing he hadn't made the offer. Who knew how much time it might take to get ready for an interview like that?

Still, as Gaby left the room—and dammit if she wasn't skipping—he couldn't get too upset. He'd spend more time in the gym, if necessary, and sleep less. He stepped onto the treadmill and set himself up for a punishing hill climb.

ZACK'S ENGINE BLEW UP during Friday's qualifying at the Pennsylvania track. Thankfully it happened near the end of his lap, and he was able to coast over the line to qualify thirty-third. Trent, as usual, was in the top ten.

The team had worked like crazy to install a replacement engine and set it up. They made it, but the mood around Zack's pit as they awaited the start of the race was grim. He knew the team was taking their cue from him, but he couldn't bring himself to smile when another major loss stared him in the face.

It didn't help that Gaby was bouncing around like an over-inflated tire, all happy because she'd suckered him into doing an interview with some magazine. *Idiot,* he castigated himself. *You're not good at that stuff.*

"I hope you're a PR witch doctor," he grumbled to Gaby as

he waited next to his car for the national anthem to start. "Because that's what it'll take to put a positive spin on this race."

"Sorry, but there's no magic," she said blithely. "You're on your own out there."

Nothing new about that, Zack thought as he circled the track a few minutes later. For some reason, the thought didn't bug him, as it usually did.

Up ahead, the lights turned green—Zack was too far back to see the flag—and he floored the accelerator.

WHEN ZACK FLEW OVER THE finish line in fourth place after as good and clean a race as a driver could hope for, Gaby whooped as loud as anyone. There had been magic out there, all right, and it had been all Zack's doing. Getaway would be thrilled. *She* was thrilled.

Zack climbed out of his car to the applause of his team. He pulled off his helmet and ran his hands through his hair, swaying slightly as he adjusted to being out of the cockpit.

"Great driving," Dave Harmon said.

Chad stepped forward. Gaby wondered if anyone else saw the way Zack stilled as he looked at his big brother.

"Chad," he said, and something in that clipped, masculine syllable tugged at Gaby's heart. She found herself willing Chad to say the right thing, her mind putting words in his mouth.

"Nice going," Chad said.

It didn't seem nearly enough to Gaby, but Zack's shoulders eased, and he and his brother gripped hands in a firm handshake.

"Our setup was slightly off, the car was pushing in the turns—we guessed the track temperatures wrong," Zack said. "If we can get a handle on that, we'll do even better next week."

Briefly, Chad's other hand clasped their joined hands. "Looks like Trent's buying the beers tonight." The youngest Matheson had finished ninth.

"I'll drink to that," Zack said. His gray eyes met Gaby's.

"Seems I'm doing my job," he said. "How about you? Got that interview arranged?"

Something in the arrogant raise of his eyebrows, tempered by the warmth in his gray eyes, made her want to laugh. Or maybe it was just the general jubilation.

"As a matter of fact, I do," she said. "Ten o'clock Tuesday morning, your place."

She expected him to balk at doing the interview in his home but he merely nodded.

"We'll start preparation on the flight back to Charlotte tonight," she said.

He squinted a little, but nodded again.

"Then we'll spend most of Monday doing more prep," she continued. She'd gone too far; he opened his mouth to protest.

"See you on the plane," she said quickly, and waltzed out of the pits.

CHAPTER FIVE

A SINGLE INTERVIEW with *Now Woman* wasn't as good as the prolonged coverage the bachelor contest would receive in America's biggest-selling weekly magazine. Not to mention on TV. But as far as Gaby was concerned, it was an excellent step toward her goal of getting Zack into the contest.

She didn't tell Zack she was still holding out for that—he'd figure it out soon enough. In the meantime, why ruin what was turning into a productive business relationship?

Although Zack was engrossed in working with his team on his car setup, he'd kept his promise, and let her call the shots on the interview preparation. They'd rehearsed answers, then she'd fired difficult questions at him in an attempt to provoke him. He was even trying to give answers that were more than the bare minimum.

The only thing he wasn't good at was turning on the charm with an interviewer. Though it frustrated her, Gaby found his inability to be shallow rather appealing.

She had high hopes for this interview, first that he would impress *Now Woman,* and second that he would find the experience not too painful. Then the next time she asked him to enter the bachelor contest, he would roll over and sign on the dotted line.

Unease flashed through her as she tried to imagine Zack rolling over for anyone.

This will work. We're getting along so well. Zack just needs a little push. She chanted the line for the thousandth time as she pressed the doorbell of Zack's French-style country home on Mountain Island Lake. Apparently he'd chosen to live away from the NASCAR enclave that clustered around the better known Lake Norman. Chad and Brianna also had a house nearby.

Zack didn't answer the door. Gaby glanced at her watch. Nine o'clock, an hour before the reporter was due.

She called Zack's cell. When he picked up, she heard a metallic thump, suspiciously like a hammer hitting metal, in the background.

"Are you at the workshop?" she asked.

"The guys and I have been working on the setup." The words were rushed, excited. "We're *this* close to finding the problem."

Gaby took a calming breath. "You have the *Now Woman* interview at ten. I'm at your place."

Zack cursed. "The thing is, there was more to the car's tightness last week than just the track temperature. We just haven't been able to figure out—"

"You need to be here now," Gaby ordered.

Silence. "I can be there in fifteen."

"You're nearer half an hour away," she said. "I don't want you killing yourself on the way."

"Your concern is touching," he teased.

Gaby took it as a good sign that he wasn't too tense. "Just get here as fast as you can, safely. In the meantime, I need to get into your house to set up for the reporter."

"Sure. Best to use the great room, I think. It has a nice view." He gave her the combination that would unlock the front door, and the code for the alarm system.

Once inside, Gaby stopped for a moment to admire the coffered ceilings, deep carpets and large windows that admitted plenty of light and made the most of the lakefront setting.

The room that had to be the great room was to the left of the entryway. It was enormous: not even the huge, overstuffed couches and coffee table the size of a small pool table could diminish it.

Gaby crossed to the French doors and soaked up the breathtaking view. The lake was a long stone's throw from the house, the water absolutely still, perfectly reflecting the trees, the jetty, the tied-up dinghy.

Gaby didn't have time to admire the outlook. She slipped the DVD she'd brought with her into the DVD player hidden in a cabinet beneath the widescreen TV, and went to make coffee.

In the kitchen—maple and granite and stainless steel—she tried not to look too hard into Zack's cupboards and drawers. The house was tidy, but not overly so. Just how she liked it.

She'd just filled the coffee press and retrieved cups and spoons when the doorbell rang. Gaby glanced at her watch— the reporter was right on time. Unlike Zack.

"Zack's been detained at the workshop," she explained to Kaye Martin, the reporter, as she ushered the woman into the great room. "He's on fire about last week's race, it's hard to drag him away from perfecting the car for this week. He should be here any moment."

Luckily, Kaye didn't seem perturbed.

"What's it like, working with such a hunk?" She examined a photo of Zack with his brothers that sat on the mantelpiece. It was the only photo in the room, and to Gaby it looked as if it was seven or eight years old.

"Uh…easy on the eyes."

Kaye laughed.

"You must meet plenty of hunks yourself, with the bachelor contest," Gaby said.

"Sure do." Kaye sat on the couch that faced out to the lake. "Unfortunately, a lot of them know just how hunky they are."

"You'll find Zack's not like that." As Gaby poured coffee, she willed him to pull up outside *right now*. As was usually the case when she tried to will him to do something, it didn't work.

They drank their first cup of coffee while they chatted

about the bachelor contest and the huge hit it was proving with the magazine's readers. It was getting plenty of coverage on TV and in the national newspapers.

"Zack should sign on for the contest," Kaye suggested. "We had another NASCAR Sprint Cup Series driver join up this week and we'll be making an announcement before Sunday's race at Watkins Glen. Readers start voting next week, so if Zack wants in, the sooner the better."

The truth—that Zack thought the contest was stupid—clearly wasn't the right answer. "Zack's well aware of the contest and the great publicity you're getting, but he's a naturally modest guy," Gaby said, and realized it was true. Zack didn't drop his big win at Daytona into conversation the way Trent would. Trent wasn't a show-off, but he naturally highlighted his successes.

A silence fell; Kaye glanced at her watch.

Come on, Zack. "I'll try his cell again," Gaby said. Her call, watched by Kaye, went straight to voice mail. "The reception can be patchy around here, he's probably a minute away," she said brightly.

He wasn't. He wasn't even fifteen minutes away. Just as Kaye was making noises about having to leave—long after Gaby herself would have given up—his pickup truck swept into the parking bay in front of the house. Only the fact that he hurried inside prevented Gaby from stabbing him with her pen.

Thank goodness he was wearing a Getaway Resorts polo, she thought as she introduced him to the reporter. He didn't have time to change.

"Sorry I'm late," he said distractedly. "My team worked through the night to find the glitch in my race car's handling. We finally cracked it half an hour ago."

"So that's not just designer stubble," Kaye said archly, eyeing Zack's unshaven chin.

"Huh?" He registered the direction of her gaze, ran his hand over his jaw. "Uh, no."

Gaby rolled her eyes. If you'd asked Trent a question like that, he'd have made some flirty rejoinder that would have won instant forgiveness for his tardiness. Zack's response highlighted how stupid the question was. Kaye's lips tightened, but she sat back down on the couch, and switched on her voice-activated recorder.

Zack slumped into the armchair opposite. From his long, slow blink, Gaby realized he was on the verge of falling asleep. Whatever adrenaline had carried him through the night, it had just run out.

She had the horrible suspicion that no matter how good his intentions toward this interview, he might forget all their preparatory work.

Give him caffeine. She poured him a coffee, though he seldom drank the stuff. He frowned when she shoved the cup into his hands, made to give it back, but when he caught her warning look he wrapped his fingers around it.

A ring at the doorbell announced the magazine's photographer, who was supposed to have arrived just as the interview wrapped up. Gaby went to let him in. Her explanation that they were running late didn't faze the man.

"Celebrities," he said with a resigned grin. "I'll set my gear up while they talk."

Back in the living room, Kaye was asking Zack some questions about his youth, easy ones designed to relax the subject. Zack looked more sleepy than relaxed, legs stretched out in front of him, eyelids heavy. He answered the questions too briefly, and Gaby had to prompt him to elaborate.

"Let's talk about your racing," Kaye said. It soon became obvious the journalist didn't know much about NASCAR. Although Gaby and Zack had rehearsed for this, tiredness seemed to have worn Zack's patience thin. He tried, but a couple of times he sounded almost snappy. The chances of a positive story in the magazine slipped a little further away with each curt response. Gaby chewed her bottom lip.

"I believe you're good friends with Kent Grosso, the son of last year's NASCAR Sprint Cup Series champion," Kaye said.

Zack nodded. "Kent's a former Sprint Cup champion himself, don't forget. I'm a couple of years older than he is, but we used to race karts together as kids and we've stayed pretty close."

Gaby had noticed Zack had strong friendships with a handful of other drivers—it was only his family he had trouble with.

"Kent must appreciate the support of friends like you, with the difficult time his family is going through," Kaye said sympathetically.

It had been a heck of a year for Kent and his parents, Dean and Patsy, who owned Cargill-Grosso Racing. Alan Cargill, the team's former owner, had been murdered in New York last December—the death of a man so beloved in the sport had shaken everyone. Then rumors had surfaced that Kent's twin sister Gina, stolen at birth and believed dead, might be alive and somehow involved in NASCAR. The press had been all over the family. They still were, going by Kaye's line of questioning.

"I don't gossip about my friends," Zack said flatly.

Gaby almost cheered. Yet she knew Zack had just made things harder. She gave him an encouraging smile.

"So, Zack." Kaye's voice was clipped. "You're still a bachelor at age thirty-four."

"Uh-huh."

Gaby could tell by his grimace he was stifling a yawn, rather than regretting his bachelor state, but fortunately the distinction bypassed Kaye.

"So, why haven't you met Ms. Right?" she asked.

"Uh…" Zack blinked again, even more slowly.

Stay awake, Gaby urged. Then wondered if it might be safer for him to fall asleep.

"You must have your share of dates," Kaye persisted.

"Sure," he said.

"Have you had many serious girlfriends?" Kaye asked.

"A couple. Don't get much time." Zack sounded about as personable as a lug nut. The reporter's eyes began to glaze over.

"So, what kind of woman will it take to win your heart?" Kaye continued gamely. "What qualities will she have?"

Yikes, they hadn't rehearsed this, since Zack wasn't part of the bachelor contest…yet. Gaby found herself listening for the answer with inordinate interest.

"I guess—" Zack ran a hand around the back of his neck, easing tired muscles "—she'll support me in my racing."

Kaye nodded encouragement.

"She'll put what I do ahead of what she does."

Excuse me? Gaby sat up straighter, tried to flash him a warning.

"Are you saying you wouldn't marry a career woman?" Kaye asked.

Zack's glance intersected with Gaby's. "Uh, my wife can have a career. Of course she can."

He probably didn't intend to sound as if he was doing the future Mrs. Zack Matheson a favor.

"It's just, while I have a window of opportunity to race NASCAR, that has to be the priority in any relationship."

Gaby groaned silently. Not only was he a lug nut, he was a Neanderthal lug nut.

Then he rubbed his eyes, and the gesture made him look oddly vulnerable.

"You need to understand that racing isn't just racing for the Mathesons," Gaby explained, trying not to sound like a desperate rescue mission. "Zack's entire family is involved in the team. Naturally, his wife would be too, to whatever extent she chose."

"Tell me about your family's history in NASCAR," Kaye said.

Zack stretched, and Gaby's gaze got hung up on his lean length, the play of muscles in his arms as he clasped his hands behind his head. Kaye appeared equally fascinated. "It all started with my father," he said. "Dad was a NASCAR champion back in the 1960s. He still has the blood of a champion in his veins, strong as ever. He's an inspiration."

Zack's respect and love for his father were obvious; Gaby thought she spied a minuscule softening in the reporter's demeanor. "Your brothers," Kaye said. "They're involved in the team, too, right?"

Uh-oh. Gaby was racking her brain for a way around certain trouble when Zack said, "In recent years, Chad and Trent have been a lot more involved than I have."

"You're the odd one out," Kaye suggested. Zack's face darkened.

"He sure is," Gaby chirped. "He's the only one who's still a bachelor." Zack's glare told her he didn't welcome a return to that topic.

"I covered Trent's wedding for the magazine." Kaye's expression turned dreamy. "What a wonderful day. We did a photo shoot of Chad and Brianna, too."

Trent's wedding had been a highlight of the NASCAR social calendar earlier this year, and the announcement of Chad's reunion with Brianna, his "secret wife," had generated many column inches in the women's magazines.

Zack gave a noncommittal grunt.

"Both your brothers married career women," Kaye observed.

"More to the point," Zack said, "they both married incredible women. Kelly is perfect for Trent, she puts a dent in his ego while still making him feel like the luckiest, happiest guy in the world."

Kaye laughed.

"And Brianna…" Zack pondered Chad's wife, and a slow smile took over his face. "She has this amazing knack for taking the pressure off Chad. He can get pretty uptight, but when Brianna's in the room, he's doesn't give a damn about anything."

"Wonderful," Kaye breathed. She wasn't talking about Chad, Gaby figured. Nope, she was looking at the way Zack's harsh face had softened, and the wistfulness in his eyes.

"Then there's Dad and Julie-Anne," Zack said. "Dad's not an easy guy, but in Julie-Anne's hands, he's like butter."

"Mmm-hmm." Kaye didn't dare do more than make an encouraging noise. Gaby contented herself with a silent nod.

"I guess," Zack said contemplatively, "my brothers and my dad found the women who were right for them. None of those women met any checklist, they probably weren't logical choices. But as it turns out, those three are the happiest guys I know."

A flash of white light broke the mood. Kaye glared at the photographer, who shrugged without apology. "Too good to miss," he said.

Zack yawned. "Are we done here?"

"Did you get that wave in Zack's hair in that shot?" Gaby asked.

"I don't have a wave in my hair," Zack said, alarmed.

"Got it," the photographer said.

"What wave?" Zack ran a hand over his head.

"Very nice," Kaye approved.

Zack got a hunted look. "There's no wave."

"It's scarcely visible," Gaby assured him.

"Then why did you want a photo of it?" he said suspiciously.

Gaby exchanged a humorous look with Kaye—the man had so little vanity, it was endearing.

"Smile, please, Zack." The photographer took a half-dozen more shots, Zack's cooperation decreasing with each one. At last, they were finished. Kaye shook Zack's hand and said, "Good luck at Watkins Glen."

Exhaustion fled, Zack's face lit up. Kaye's mouth dropped open at the sheer beauty of him; Gaby knew just how she felt. Carefully, the photographer lifted his camera, snapped a couple of shots without the flash.

"I won't need luck," Zack said. "Not with the work we just put in on the car."

Yes! Somehow, they'd ended on a high. As Gaby escorted Kaye and the photographer to the door she felt a surge of the kind of relief heart patients must feel when brought back to life by a defibrillator.

"Interesting man," Kaye said as she stepped outside.

"He sure is." Gaby wondered if she meant *interesting cool,* or *interesting psycho.*

"Pity he's not in the bachelor contest," the reporter said. "I could do a major article on him then."

Gaby turned cold, despite the sunshine. "Your editor told me this would be a five-page profile." That was why she'd busted her butt, gone through all this stress.

Kaye grimaced. "We don't have the space. The advertisers are supporting the bachelor contest, and that's where our coverage is going."

"So, how big will this article be?" Gaby tried to hide her dismay.

The reporter shrugged. "A page, tops. We'll give him a decent photograph."

All that effort in exchange for a measly page, doubtless tucked in the back of the magazine behind the bachelors. Sandra and Getaway were expecting a major feature. Because Gaby had told them to. And after that, there would be…nothing. She knew without talking to Zack that he hadn't enjoyed the interview. So he wasn't about to announce his candidacy in the bachelor contest.

"That's disappointing," Gaby said. She heard the weakness in her voice and despised it. What had Sandra said? *I need someone who'll fight for my business.*

Gaby was letting *Now Woman* renege on its commitment, when the editor and the journalist surely knew they'd never have been given so much of Zack's time on such short notice, at this stage in the season, unless it was for a major return. She had also let Zack renege on his commitment, because she had wanted him to get that car right, and because his fatigue had tugged at her heartstrings.

Dammit, right now she didn't *deserve* that promotion.

Fight, she told herself. *Not just for Sandra's business, but for yourself, for your future, for your peace of mind.* Determination trickled into her veins. Not enough. *If you don't fight this battle, no one else will.* Resolve built, becoming a flood that swept her forward.

"That's not acceptable." Gaby amended her earlier comment to the journalist, her tone clipped.

"There's nothing I can do," Kaye said, her smile friendly but firm.

"There's always something." Gaby tugged the front door closed behind her. "What if Zack signs on for the bachelor contest?"

Kaye's eyes lit up. "He didn't seem overly interested."

"If I can persuade him," Gaby persisted, "will you give us the cover?"

The request went beyond what they'd agreed with the magazine, but as far as she knew, Zack had never had the cover of a women's magazine. Unlike Trent.

Kaye pursed her lips. "I'd need to talk to my editor. But Zack would sure spice up the contest—he's a bit of a dark horse."

You can say that again. "He won't enter unless we get the cover," Gaby said firmly.

Kaye hesitated. "I think we can do that—I'll call you when I'm back at the office."

Gaby shook the reporter's hand with a determination that her marshmallow-me didn't recognize. *Hold that thought. And go back inside to Zack, ready to fight with everything you've got.*

CHAPTER SIX

AMAZING HOW THE DECISION to fight for her life crystallized Gaby's thoughts. By the time she reached the great room, she had a full battle strategy. She wasn't entirely proud of it, but she was confident it would work.

She found Zack flopped on the couch, his head thrown back, eyes closed. Lines of tiredness ran from his nose to the corners of his mouth, and for a moment Gaby thought he'd fallen asleep. He held up a hand as she approached. "I know, I know. I screwed up."

Gaby sucked in a breath. "Actually, you did okay."

He opened his eyes. "Really?" He looked wary. "What did I say?"

"But you almost screwed up," Gaby continued. "I can't go through this stress every time we have a media interview."

"Then let's not do any more interviews." He gave her a hopeful look. "Now that my driving and my car are back on track…"

"One fourth-place finish doesn't equal back on track."

"That's not what you told that reporter," he said.

"I was putting you in a positive light."

"Maybe," he said, "the light is real. Like the sun. Not something that's going to switch off next week." He tsked at his own garbled metaphor and said, "So you think the article will be all right?"

"You're going to be on the cover," Gaby said.

"Wow." He sat up. "The cover." He ran a hand over his face. "Maybe I should have shaved."

Gaby looked at the darkness of shadow accentuating the strong line of his jaw. Every woman who saw that magazine would drool. She was having a hard time refraining from drooling herself, and she was mad at him.

She licked her lips, in case a stray fleck of drool had escaped. "Getaway doesn't mind the unshaven look," she said. "They think it sends a message that their hotels are places where you can really relax."

He rolled his eyes at the PR-speak.

"You nearly killed that interview, but only just," she said. "What happened to all that preparation we did?"

"I've been up all night," he began.

"You have a car chief and a bunch of mechanics to fix your car, but no one else could do this interview. You should have gone to bed so you could keep your promise to me."

"What's the problem?" he said. "I admit I made some mistakes, but like you said, it went okay."

"We weren't aiming for *okay*," she said. "Things have to change."

"There's not much chance I'll be up all night working on the car again…."

Gaby crossed to the DVD player and started it. She used the remote to turn on the TV. "Watch this—it was picked up by all the national networks last night."

Color flashed onto the TV screen, a segment of a popular breakfast show.

"Today we get to meet some of the candidates for *Now Woman* magazine's Bachelor of the Year," the presenter said.

That snagged Zack's attention. "What the—?"

"Hush," Gaby ordered, her eyes glued to the parade of drivers on the screen.

"Idiots," Zack said.

She glared at him. "Publicity-savvy, you mean. Look at

Garrett Clark." She pointed as the camera zoomed in on the handsome driver wearing his sponsor's T-shirt. "Country Bread's logo on national TV. He didn't even have to win a race."

Garrett was chatting to a group of admiring females. He certainly was handsome, Gaby had to admit, with those chocolate-brown eyes and those—

"Hey," Zack said. "What are you gawping at?"

"I'm *watching* a driver who understands PR at work."

He stabbed a finger at the TV. "You *like* Garrett Clark?"

"I respect his abilities," she said primly. Then, as it dawned on her that Zack's mile-wide competitive streak was coming into play, she added, "Yeah, he's cute."

"He's a womanizer," Zack said.

Gaby laughed at the old-fashioned term, and he scowled. "I thought he was a friend of yours," she said.

"He is," Zack said. "I'm not a woman, I'm safe with him."

"It makes sense that a great-looking guy like Garrett Clark *would* be a womanizer," she said thoughtfully.

Zack stood and walked over to the TV. He stood in front of it, blocking her view. "You told me I'm a hottie," he pointed out. "But I'm not a womanizer."

Gaby's hormones leapt; she slapped them down. This was business. "Looks aren't everything. Women like men who talk to them." She craned to see the screen around him.

"Okay, what do you want to talk about?"

The belligerence in Zack's voice startled her, even though it was what she'd been pushing for. "Excuse me?"

He switched off the TV. "I can do the weather," he said. "Or NASCAR. Movies, books. Just say the word."

Gaby's stomach fluttered. Zack definitely didn't like that she thought Garrett Clark was cute. "You think that's all Garrett talks about? Superficial stuff?"

Zack snorted. "The guy's about as deep as a puddle at the top of a banked track."

"Interesting," Gaby murmured, and was rewarded with a deeper frown. "What if I want to talk about the Bachelor of the Year contest?"

His mouth firmed. "Sure, we can talk about that. It's a load of garbage."

"Garrett doesn't seem to think so." She looked suggestively at the blank screen.

Zack bristled. "I'm not entering that stupid contest. I don't need to prove I'm a heck of a lot more interesting than Garrett Clark."

She let her brows draw together in dubious assessment.

"I *am*," he said, warningly.

"Uh-huh." She wandered to the table and poured another coffee from the press. She took a swig of the cold liquid. Now or never. "Actually Zack, you do need to prove you're a better catch than Garrett. I entered you in the Bachelor of the Year contest."

Zack jerked backward. "You *what?*"

"Have you seen how much exposure these guys are getting? The contest has been on all the major networks, and it will be again. It's sponsored by the biggest-selling weekly magazine in the country, and the daily newspapers are picking up stories all the time."

"I'm a NASCAR driver, not a-a beauty king." He sat down on the couch, disgusted.

"You had one good race," Gaby said. "Not enough for Getaway, not enough for the media and certainly not enough for your own satisfaction."

"The bachelor contest sure as hell won't give me any satisfaction," he said.

"We can't keep lurching from one interview, one race, to the next and hoping we don't screw up too badly. The contest gives us week after week of strong, positive coverage, whatever else happens."

"You said yourself I don't have the social skills of drivers like Garrett Clark and Trent," he pointed out. "What makes you think I'll get positive coverage?"

"I saw an indication of what you can do at today's interview. We'll build on that." She sucked in a breath and stood over him in an attempt to intimidate. "I plan to put you through charm school."

He stared up at her. "Huh?"

"The first lesson is to stop confusing *huh* and *uh* for conversation," she snapped. "From now on, I want multiword sentences. Even some multisyllable words."

"Ne-ver go-ing to hap-pen," he enunciated clearly.

"I mean it, Zack. I need you to commit one hundred percent to the bachelor contest, and that means changing your attitude to just about everything."

He got to his feet, terminating her brief height advantage. "I told you, the only thing I'll commit to one hundred percent is my racing."

Frustrated, Gaby paced the room. Couldn't he see that success in the bachelor contest might actually help his racing? He needed a confidence boost. "I already told the reporter you're in."

"Then it's your job to get me out," he said.

She eyeballed him. "No."

"What are you going to do, *make* me do the contest?" He laughed, and it was the last straw.

Gaby flung hesitancy to the winds…along with her professional ethics. Zack didn't give a damn about anyone else, why should she give a damn about what he wanted?

She sat carefully on the couch he'd just vacated, ignoring the magnetism of his presence, and folded her hands in her lap. Steeling herself.

"What?" Zack asked, suspicious.

She decided to overlook the single-syllable sentence. "We both know there's something else you're willing to put a hundred percent into."

"No, there's not." His gaze flickered toward the door.

"And we both know this comeback isn't just about your racing," she said silkily.

"Of course it is." But he ran a finger around the back of his shirt collar, and Gaby knew she had him.

"Your family," she said. "They're more important to you than your racing, but if possible, you're doing even worse with them than you are on the track."

The heat of his glare could have melted pavement. "You don't know what you're talking about."

"Sit down, Zack," she said. "I plan to make you an offer you can't refuse."

ZACK SAT ON THE OTHER end of the couch. Because he wanted to, not because Gaby said so. Because he was so damn tired after more than twenty-four hours on his feet.

He didn't know how she'd come up with her theory about his family—a lucky guess, most likely—but he wasn't about to discuss it.

"You will attend charm school and graduate with flying colors," she said. "Then you will participate in every event, every interview you're asked to do in relation to the bachelor contest, and you'll do it with charm, flair and…and sexiness." She colored, but her tone was firm.

"So far I'm finding this pretty easy to refuse," he said, relieved. For a minute there, she'd had him going with her pseudo insights.

"In exchange for your cooperation," she said deliberately, "I will provide additional services."

He raised an eyebrow and smirked. She shot him a look that said *how puerile,* and continued, "Your comeback is as much about coming back into your family as it is into NASCAR. Probably more. But it's not working."

"You think?" he sneered.

"Do you have any idea why that is?" Her clear blue eyes met his.

And, dammit, he was so tired, so damn susceptible, he found himself saying, "Matheson Racing is all about winning."

"By which you mean, *being a Matheson* is all about winning."

"If I wanted psychoanalysis, I'd go see Kelly." He added rudely, "She's a lot better at it than you are."

To his irritation, Gaby smiled with what looked like genuine sympathy. "You really are a mess."

"I'm fine," he muttered. He *had* been fine until she started in on him. He never should have agreed to this morning's interview.

"I believe you go into conversations with your family with good intentions—at least half the time. But something always goes wrong."

She was right, half the time he did. The other times, he was too riled to make the effort.

"I've seen the hopeful look you get on your face when you talk to your dad, your brothers."

Heat suffused Zack's jaw. "Don't be stupid." She made him sound like a five-year-old seeking his daddy's approval, his love. Yeah, okay, so he wanted some kind of connection with his dad and his brothers. But he didn't *need* it, and if this season didn't work out, he could go back to Atlanta and resume his pattern of occasional communication with his folks.

Something twisted inside him at the thought.

He shot Gaby a look of intense dislike and considered having her fired.

"If it's any consolation," she said, "your problems with your folks aren't all your fault."

"Gee, thanks," he said sarcastically

"Even when you're on your best behavior—which, frankly, isn't that great—your family is guilty of judging what you say and do in the light of past grudges."

She'd noticed that, too? That no matter what he did, no matter how pure his motives, someone took it the wrong way? Zack shoved his hands in his pockets. "Go on," he growled.

"I have a solution."

The leaping sensation in his chest was totally unexpected. He couldn't speak.

"I will work with you on improving your image with your family," Gaby said.

The soaring hope—because that was what this feeling must be—plummeted. Zack cursed himself for his naiveté. Had he really expected Gaby to have the answer to a decades-old problem?

"A PR campaign," she elaborated. "One aimed at showing your family you're a Matheson just like them, and without you the family is less than it should be."

"You want to *spin* me to my family?" Zack said, outraged. "You're nuts."

"I admit you're driving me crazy," she said. "But putting you in the bachelor contest will fix that." She leaned forward, and the movement parted her blouse. Zack got a glimpse of creamy skin. He jerked his gaze away.

"I can't fix the psychology of what's going on in your family, but I can help change perceptions," she said. "Once you change someone's viewpoint, then they reevaluate everything, and react to words and behaviors, in the light of that new view."

He tried to follow her reasoning. "You're saying that if Dad and my brothers think I'm a nice guy, they won't jump on everything I say?"

That did have some appeal. Right now, every time he made the tiniest progress with his family, he'd open his mouth and ruin it. Which possibly came down to those deep-rooted perceptions. Maybe the reason he got along so well with his sisters-in-law was because they didn't prejudge every communication.

"They'll see everything differently," Gaby agreed.

Despite the fact he was mad with her and had every reason to be, the idea proved incredibly seductive. Zack found himself leaning toward her.

"It's not all perception," she said. "You'll need to change some behaviors, but if you know what you're trying to achieve you can avoid a knee-jerk reaction when people say something you don't like."

That made sense. "And you think a PR campaign can do all this?"

"I know it can." She sat back, sensing victory. "It will mean me spending a lot more time with you. For a while, at least, I'll need to be present during most of your family interactions."

Zack made the surprising discovery he could live with spending more time with Gaby. But what she was proposing was too weird. "I'm too busy for this."

"How much time, how much race focus do you think you lose to fretting about your family?" she demanded.

A lot. Looking at Gaby in profile, Zack wondered why he'd never noticed the stubborn tilt of her chin. Her soft voice, with that edge of nervousness, had lulled him into a false impression that she was a pushover.

She didn't wait for him to articulate his answer. "When you feel confident you have your personal life under control, your racing should improve."

How many times this season had the solitude of the No. 548 car proven an overfertile time to ponder his grievances? Could those negative thoughts affect his racing? Of course they could—everyone knew racing was a head game.

"How would this work?" he asked reluctantly, scarcely able to believe he was considering manipulating his family. *Why not? Nothing else has worked.*

"We'll tackle both campaigns at once—the bachelor contest and your family. You will pay meticulous attention to the charm school lessons I give, *which*—" she fixed him with a firm eye just as he began to protest "—will be as relevant to your family situation as they are to the contest."

Zack harrumphed.

"You will make every effort with the contest, and in all circumstances you will behave as I tell you."

"The power has gone to your head," he said.

"I'm not joking."

Zack had been so wrapped up in his own troubles, he hadn't realized until now that the lengths she was prepared to go to were extreme.

"Why are you so hot on this?" he asked. "You're going way beyond the call of duty."

"It's my—"

"Your job, right." He twisted to face her. "I don't buy it."

Her gaze slid away. "This is about you, not me."

"I'm not going along with this crazy scheme unless I know what's in it for you." He saw the way her eyes lit up at the thought of him giving in. Yeah, well, he was desperate. "Tell me," he ordered, "or it's no dice."

Her lips clamped together.

Zack picked up the remote control and turned the TV on, ignoring her. He found a cartoon channel, and settled back against the couch.

"Fine," Gaby said tightly at last.

"I'd prefer you to use multisyllable words," he said helpfully. "You need to set a good example for me."

She glared. "I want to run Motor Media Group while Sandra's on maternity leave."

Whatever Zack had expected, it wasn't that. He turned off the TV. "That's a big job."

She huffed. "You don't think I can do it?"

"I have no idea. But I haven't seen Sandra look at you as if *she* thinks you can do it." Zack was so used to seeing doubt in his family's faces, he recognized it easily in others.

"I need to prove my capabilities," Gaby admitted.

He mulled that over. "You think if you keep me in line, Sandra will give you the job?"

"You're my client, you're the obvious place to start."

"So your offer to help me with my family isn't about me at all?" The thought rankled. Dumb, since he was used to playing second, or third, fiddle. "This is all about you."

"I do want you to fix things with your family," she said. "But, yes, my main concern is getting that job."

"Why do you want it? Is it the money?"

Gaby laced her fingers in her lap. "Kind of. My parents were quite old when they had me—Mom was forty-six. They're not in great health, physically or financially. They can meet their own needs, but they've made it clear there's unlikely to be much left for me when they go. I need to make provision for myself."

"Do they live around here?"

She shook her head. "In Nashville. I don't have any other family."

"You'll probably get married one day." Zack scanned her slim curves, the feminine sweep of her lashes above blue eyes, the bow of her mouth. "Your husband will help support you."

"I already tried that," she said coolly.

"You've been married?" Something primeval—possessiveness, protectiveness, he didn't know what—swept over Zack.

"Engaged," she said. "It was a painful lesson in not relying on someone else to take care of me."

"What did he do to you?" One look at the quiver in Gaby's lips and Zack had an urge to pound the guy's head into the pavement.

Her face shut down, the way his own often did. "I answered your question about what I want out of this, you don't need to know anything else. You just need to agree to enter the bachelor contest, give it a hundred-percent effort. In return, I'll help manage the impressions you give your family, the same way I manage your media impressions. Only better," she added, "because now you'll be cooperating."

Zack briefly entertained a scenario in his head where he and his family laughed and chatted and bantered around a

Thanksgiving table. Too sappy. He dismissed the image and conjured another one, where he and his folks were civil to each other, where every conversation wasn't a minefield.

Even that was a vast improvement.

He let out a breath. "I'll do it," he said. "I'm in your hands."

Something electric crackled in the air, left his heart thumping.

Gaby put a hand to her chest as if her heart was playing up, too. "See you in charm school."

CHAPTER SEVEN

"MIND YOUR MANNERS, and don't go on about NASCAR," Brady Matheson ordered his sons, who were sprawled around his living room on the Wednesday evening between the Pennsylvania and Watkins Glen races. "It's a sensitive issue for Amber." But all he got for his trouble was three pairs of rolled eyes. His daughters-in-law were more polite and nodded obediently.

"She's your stepsister," he reminded them all unnecessarily. *And she's my stepdaughter.* "She's part of our family." He added hastily, "That doesn't mean you can go arguing with her or insulting her or getting her dander up like you do with each other."

Dammit, he hadn't been this nervous in years. Yet again, he wondered if it was a wise idea having the boys here while he met Amber Blake, Julie-Anne's daughter, for the first time.

Julie-Anne was desperate for the meeting to go well, which put Brady on edge. She'd insisted Amber would feel less threatened if she was in a big group, rather than one-on-one.

Threatened. Brady cursed under his breath. He wanted to like his stepdaughter, he really did. But she sounded neurotic. She'd better not try to come between him and Julie-Anne.

Yet she already had. Julie-Anne had insisted on going to the airport alone yesterday to greet her daughter. Not unreasonable—except mother and daughter had spent the night at Julie-Anne's cottage in Charlotte. It was the first night Brady and Julie-Anne had spent apart since they married.

He'd missed his wife.

And Julie-Anne had missed Amber the past few years, more than most people knew. Brady sighed. He needed to be the better guy about this.

"Dad, we'll be on our best behavior," Zack promised, unusually cooperative.

Brady snorted. "With you, that means you'll either ignore her or you'll blow up at her."

Dammit, he always said the wrong thing to Zack. Sure enough, his middle son's eyes hardened, his chin jutted. Brady braced himself for an argument he didn't need right now. Sometimes he thought life was easier when Zack wasn't talking to the family.

Gaby, Zack's PR rep, put a hand on Zack's arm. He glared down at her, but it seemed to distract him from retaliating.

Brady let out a relieved breath. He hadn't realized Zack was dating his PR rep—the boy was secretive—but if she managed to curb his moodiness, Brady was all in favor.

The crunch of tires on the gravel driveway alerted him. "They're here."

He hurried onto the porch. Amber got out of the car, and he was relieved to see she looked a lot like Julie-Anne, with her long dark hair and curvy figure. If she was like her mother personality-wise, this wouldn't be so bad.

Julie-Anne planted a quick kiss on Brady's mouth; as always, he wanted more. "Darling, this is Amber," she said.

Brady shook the girl's hand. "It's a pleasure to meet you." Awkwardly, he leaned in and kissed her cheek.

She stiffened a bit, then smiled. "You, too, Brady."

"I, uh, I got you something." He reached over to the porch swing and handed her a large, white teddy bear holding a Welcome to Charlotte sign.

Right away, he knew it was a bad choice. Sure, she thanked him, but he could see from her raised, then quickly lowered, eyebrows that she thought he was crazy buying her a stuffed animal.

"Libby, the receptionist at the race team, it was her idea," he explained hurriedly.

Behind him, Trent groaned. "Dad, everyone knows Libby has a stuffed animal fetish. Most grown women don't want a teddy bear."

Brady felt heat at the back of his neck.

"It's sweet," Amber insisted. "It really is."

"Hi, I'm Trent." Trent stepped forward and shook her hand, which at least took the pressure off Brady for a minute.

He and Amber had talked on the phone a couple of times, but it didn't seem to make this any easier. Not when Julie-Anne was hovering anxiously, worried he might offend the girl.

He cleared his throat. "Come inside and meet the other boys."

Thankfully, his sons managed to dredge up impeccable manners from somewhere, and Brady started to breathe easier.

"Are you pleased to be home?" Zack asked Amber.

She glanced around the spacious, high-ceilinged living room. "Charlotte hasn't been my home in a long time." Obviously realizing how ungracious she sounded, she blushed. "But I'm pleased to see Mom again."

"Not half as thrilled as I am to see you, honey." Julie-Anne put an arm around her daughter. Amber didn't exactly melt into her mother's touch. Julie-Anne was right, Brady thought—her daughter was still holding on to some resentment.

As Julie-Anne served the meal, a Tex-Mex feast that would appeal to everyone, Amber watched her mom's interactions with him like a hawk. But she was pleasant to everyone else.

It'll take time, Brady told himself. *But we'll win her over.* They had to, for Julie-Anne's sake.

AMBER SIPPED HER BEER, smiled politely in response to something Zack Matheson—her stepbrother—said, and wondered how soon she could get out of here. She needed to take a long walk, clear her head. Zack seemed nice enough, and so did his brothers, but who really knew? More importantly, who knew what Brady Matheson was really like? If he was as gruff as his demeanor suggested, there was every chance Amber's mom had made a terrible mistake. Again.

Amber eyed Julie-Anne, saw the nervousness in her jerky movements as she passed around the plates of food. Was her mom merely worried about this reunion, or was her anxiety due to something more sinister?

I should have come home sooner. Julie-Anne's announcement of her engagement to Brady at the end of last year had set off alarm bells, and Amber had begun the process of extracting herself from her contract with her eco-adventure tour company employer. Then, in January, Julie-Anne had e-mailed that the engagement was off. Out of consideration to her employer during the busy New Year period, Amber canceled her trip. Only to learn a couple of weeks later that Brady and Julie-Anne had run off to Las Vegas to get married.

Did he browbeat her into it?

Julie-Anne had e-mailed to say how ecstatic she was, but Amber wasn't convinced. It had taken a while to get out of her commitments, but she was here to see for herself. If she discovered Brady was anything like Julie-Anne's first husband, Billy Blake, the man Amber could scarcely bear to acknowledge as her father...

"Amber, will you be looking for work here in Charlotte?" Brady asked.

She couldn't gauge his tone, and that worried her. If Brady was like her father, he was smarter about hiding it than Billy had been. "I'm not sure how long I'll stay," she admitted.

She'd been traveling for years, it would be hard to settle. Even if, sometimes, she craved to be somewhere called home.

"You'll have to come by Matheson Racing," Zack said. "Have Dad show you around. He started the team thirty years ago, back when he was racing himself, so as tour guides go he's pretty inspiring." His cheery tone seemed forced. Gaby—his girlfriend?—gave him an encouraging smile.

"Thanks, son." Brady sounded surprised at the compliment. He turned to Amber. "I'd be happy to show you around the team headquarters."

"Uh, I'm not sure what my plans are." As if she would be so frantically busy in this town where she no longer knew anyone that she wouldn't have time to visit the team. Still, it was more polite than, *No way am I setting foot in that place.*

The conversation moved on; Amber was content to observe.

Julie-Anne started gathering empty plates. "I'll serve dessert."

Brady stood. "I'll help you, sweetheart."

Amber leaped to her feet. "I'll help, Mom."

Julie-Anne looked from her husband to her daughter. Amber had the ridiculous urge to put up her hand and beg, *Pick me. This time, pick me.*

"It won't need three of us," Julie-Anne said. "Amber, I'd love it if you could help."

Amber couldn't help shooting a look of triumph at Brady as she followed her mom to the kitchen. *Childish,* she scolded herself.

"Darling, you're coping wonderfully," Julie-Anne said as she pulled the peach cobbler, Amber's childhood favorite, from the oven. "I know the Matheson men can be overwhelming when you get them all in one room."

"Any more testosterone and I'd be in danger of growing hairs on my chest," Amber agreed.

A tiny joke, but Julie-Anne laughed more heartily than it warranted. "So…what do you think?" she asked.

She meant *of Brady,* but Amber chose a wider interpretation. "Zack seems harmless," she said.

Julie-Anne blinked. "Zack? You're right, he's a sweetie, though not everyone is smart enough to see that."

"Trent…it's hard to believe that much charm could be genuine." Amber's father had apparently been a real charmer himself, when it suited him.

Julie-Anne didn't appear to get the parallel. Her eyes

softened. "Sweetie, you're a cynic. Trent's a doll, through and through." She reached out and touched Amber's cheek. Amber jerked away, even though she wanted to stay there and enjoy the caress. Julie-Anne's expression turned hurt.

"Chad seems competent," Amber hurried on. "He's very like Brady." In manner, as well as looks. Chad wasn't gruff, like Brady, but she'd bet he and his dad shared a lot of attitudes. Chad's wife, Brianna, appeared besotted with him—and vice versa—but they hadn't been together long.

Julie-Anne obviously sensed the unspoken criticism, because her voice cooled as she said, "Chad *is* very like his father. Which is the highest compliment I can pay."

Amber began counting plates out from the cupboard that her mom had indicated and then moved on to the opinion her mom was really waiting for. "Brady seems... strong."

The sigh Julie-Anne let out sounded more like an infatuated sixteen-year-old than a middle-aged woman. "He's like a rock."

Amber frowned. "Immovable?"

"Dependable," Julie-Anne said. "Reliable, protective. If Brady seems offhand with you, it's because he's protecting me."

"What does he think I'm going to do?" Amber demanded, stung.

"Nothing," Julie-Anne soothed her. "It's just, he knows you haven't been back in a while, and he's worried about whether we'll all get along."

Amber pffed as she set out the plates on the counter. More likely, Brady was worried someone might see through his loving-husband act. She clamped down on the uncharitable thought. Maybe Brady *was* a loving husband. Maybe.

"Give him the benefit of the doubt." As if she'd read Amber's mind, Julie-Anne turned pleading. "Be happy for me."

Because my *happiness was so important to you? So important that you abandoned me?* Amber quashed the bitter accusation. Now wasn't the time to have that argument. She doubted there ever would be a time, if she wanted any kind of relationship with her mother.

It doesn't matter that she chose my father over me, I don't care. She repeated the mantra that had sustained her through the lonely years, gradually creating a protective shell around her.

"Brady is nothing like Billy," Julie-Anne said quietly. "I promise."

"They both drove race cars." Then Amber burst out, "I can't believe you're back in this world, after everything that happened."

Julie-Anne pulled a serving spoon from a drawer. "I love racing, and I have a lot of friends in the sport. You used to love it, too."

Amber shuddered. "But *he*—"

"NASCAR didn't make your father what he was," Julie-Anne interrupted. "If anything, it gave him a reason to be a better man."

They were never going to agree on that. Amber switched tactics. "You don't look happy."

"I don't—?" Julie-Anne gaped. "Sweetheart, I adore Brady, he's made me happier than I've ever been in my life. Apart from when you were born," she added. Too late.

She dug a serving spoon into the cobbler. Steam rose from the golden dessert.

"You can't expect me to just accept your judgment of him," Amber said.

Her mom paused, spoon in the air. "Why not?"

"Mom, you made a huge mistake the first time around."

"And therefore every decision I make must be equally faulty?" Julie-Anne's eyes flashed. "It's been eleven years since Billy died, and you'll notice I didn't exactly rush in to another relationship. What I have with Brady—"

"He swept you off your feet," Amber said.

To her surprise, her mom laughed. "He did no such thing. You've never seen a man try harder to avoid falling in love."

Which was even worse, Amber thought. "I just want to be sure you're happy."

Julie-Anne's shoulders eased. "I am. Trust me. And accept my marriage."

How about Amber hops on the next plane back to Katmandu, instead? The usual wanderlust didn't kick in at the prospect. Instead she found herself saying, "I'll try."

From the dining room, she heard one of her stepbrothers make a reference to last week's race, and immediately, loud, assertive voices weighed in with their opinions. Amber wrapped her arms around herself.

"And I hope you can eventually get over your downer on NASCAR," Julie-Anne said. "It's a big part of my life, Amber."

Amber jerked a nod.

"I want you to visit the team headquarters," Julie-Anne said. "See for yourself, it's just a place where people work. Decent people, whose families matter to them."

"Mom, I don't want to go there."

Her mother's expression turned stern. "I know it'll be hard for you, Amber, but I'm your mother, and if I tell you to get yourself to that team headquarters that's exactly what you'll do."

Amber's instinctive, conflicting reactions both made her feel about ten years old. Flounce from the room, or latch on to that maternal order as if she had no choice.

Brady stuck his head around the doorway. "Everything okay?"

He's keeping tabs on her, just like Billy did. Amber shivered, despite the heat of the kitchen. Her mom would never see the similarity between Brady and Billy unless Amber showed her the truth. She needed to catch Brady unawares, when he wasn't putting on a social face. Anyone could play Mr. Nice Guy for a couple of hours at a stretch.

She swallowed her trepidation and said, "Brady, I need to earn some money while I'm back in town. Any chance you can find me something to do at that engine company of yours?"

Brady looked dismayed. "Uh, sure."

"Thanks." She gave him a sunny smile. The engine company had to be less intimidating than the team headquarters. And it would keep her closer to her stepfather. *I'm on to you.*

Brady took the first of the dessert bowls from Julie-Anne and carried them to the dining room.

"Thank you, sweetie," Julie-Anne said to Amber. "That was a good thing to do."

Amber shrugged.

"We should talk about Billy," Julie-Anne said. "Soon." She touched Amber's arm, and once more, Amber moved away.

"I don't want to even hear his name," she said.

Julie-Anne looked as if she would argue. Then she raised her hands in surrender.

And no wonder. Because she couldn't come out of any conversation about Billy Blake without looking like a mother who hadn't loved her daughter enough.

SOMETHING AS PERSONAL AS charm school demanded a strictly impersonal locale. The Matheson Racing headquarters wasn't suitable, because someone was bound to figure out what they were up to. So Gaby asked the Getaway Hotel in Charlotte to provide a room she and Zack could use.

She had meant a meeting space. But when they arrived at the hotel, they were given the key to a room on one of the bedroom floors.

"The business center is fully occupied," the receptionist said. "But the room we've given you has a table and chairs."

Which was fine. All Gaby had to do was ignore the king-size bed. Zack wandered the space, apparently unfazed by the six-foot expanse of duvet.

"Not a bad room," he said. Maybe because she'd helped him deflect a couple of arguments during yesterday's dinner at Brady's house, Zack had turned up on time, and his face didn't bear its usual guarded demeanor.

Gaby was more nervous than her pupil, thanks to the bedroom factor. *I'm just tired.* Last night, after that dinner at Brady's, she'd actually dreamed about Zack. Though it had been fleeting, just a few seconds of REM action, she hadn't been able to put it out of her mind.

"Are you okay?" Zack had noticed her fidgeting.

"We need more air in here." She fanned her face as she checked the thermostat. She turned the temperature down, and heard the whir of air-conditioning. "Do you want a coffee?"

"Let's just get this over with." Zack sat on the end of the bed.

"Not there." Her sharp tone drew a curious glance from him. "Over here." She indicated the round table near the window, flanked by two velvet-upholstered chairs.

Zack obediently relocated; Gaby took the chair opposite. She straightened her notepad on the table in front of her.

"*Now Woman* suggests several criteria for readers to consider when they vote for the Bachelor of the Year," she began. "I plan to cover each of those criteria in our training, plus we'll do some role-playing to prepare for some of the public events related to the contest."

Zack shuddered.

"First up, your appearance," she said.

His eyebrows lifted. "There's something wrong with my appearance? You said I'm a hottie."

Was he ever going to let her forget that?

"It's not about looks, it's about presentation." Gaby scanned him and couldn't fault his well-cut hair, which looked a little lighter than usual, thanks to the sun streaming in the tinted hotel room window. Nor was there any problem with the breadth of his shoulders, or the slate-colored polo shirt that deepened the color of his eyes.

"Your hands need attention," she said.

Zack looked down at his fingers as if he'd never seen them before. "What's wrong with them?"

"You've obviously been in the workshop." Most NASCAR

Sprint Cup Series drivers never worked on their race car. That's what they had highly specialized teams for. But Zack, she knew, took a hands-on interest, literally. The worse his results, the more engine oil made its way on to his hands.

"There's nothing wrong with my hands." He shoved them in her direction. "Take a look."

At first glance, they were clean, but something suggested he'd handled an engine in recent times.

Gaby took his right hand in hers. *Mistake.* The slight pressure of his fingers branded her palm, and when her thumb brushed his, sensation feathered all the way up her arm.

"There." The word came out a half gasp. Carefully, she pointed to Zack's index finger. "Engine oil around the cuticle."

"Around the what?"

She ran a fingernail over the offending area. He jerked away. "No one—" he cleared his throat "—no-one will see that without a microscope."

"It doesn't matter if people can't specifically see oil, it's the overall impression that counts. In a tough competition like Bachelor of the Year, where you have a bunch of guys determined to win, details matter." She sat back. "Women appreciate clean hands. You should wear gloves in the workshop."

He gaped. "You're kidding."

"Latex disposables will do the job."

"I can't wear gloves in the workshop."

"You're scared the other boys will laugh at you?" she taunted.

"I'm not scared," he snapped.

"Good, then gloves it is. I'll bring a box in on Monday."

Zack glared at her.

"I notice you often wear jeans," she said.

"There's no engine oil on my jeans," he said ominously.

"I'm sure you're right." No way was she about to inspect them! "But some of the bachelor contest events will call for more sartorial style."

"I'm a race car driver, not a Ken doll."

"No one would ever mistake you for a Ken doll," she said. Nope, Zack Matheson was all living, breathing, red-blooded man. "If you don't have other clothes, I can arrange for a selection—"

"I have other clothes," he growled.

"Excellent, I'll look forward to seeing them." Gaby's knees were close to meltdown—she was proud that none of her nerves showed in her voice. Something about working for Zack toughened her up, and she liked it.

"The good news is," she said, "I watched you last night and your table manners are perfect."

His grunt suggested he was partially mollified.

"And you're strong on courtesies like opening doors for women, standing when they come into a room and so on."

"Dad was big on that stuff," he admitted. "When we were teenagers he told us good manners would get us more girls, which was enough to get our buy-in."

"Surely you never needed more girls?" She said it without thinking. Hastily she added, "I mean, you or your brothers."

Too late, he was grinning. "How many girls do you think are enough?"

CHAPTER EIGHT

"HOW MANY GIRLS DO *you* think are enough?" Gaby challenged him right back.

"When I was a teenager?" he said. "Or now?"

The atmosphere thickened and prickled like thousands of tiny needles.

Gaby squirmed, finally deciding retreat was safest. She glanced down at her notes. "But, um, although you have a strong grasp of courtesy, your personal projection leaves something to be desired."

"Are we talking about that PowerPoint update we did for Getaway?"

"We're talking about your personality." She was pretty sure he knew that.

He tilted his chair back on two legs. "Tell me what's wrong with me," he invited.

"You know darn well you're about as friendly as a bear that's been run over by a race car."

He scratched his head at the bizarre analogy. "Are you going to nag me about smiling again?"

"Smiling is part of the issue, but it's also about showing an interest in other people."

He looked at her blankly. This was the essence of Zack's problem, Gaby realized. Until he stopped being so wrapped up in his own troubles, he wouldn't connect with others.

"The whole world doesn't revolve around your racing," she said.

"The bit that matters does."

She rolled her eyes. "Zack, for starters, when a reporter interviews you, you need to ask them a couple of questions, too."

"I'm not the one writing an article," he protested. "What's the point?"

"The point is, when you take time to forge a two-way connection, everything goes better. That applies to your family, as well as the media."

He looked mystified. Gaby sighed. "No wonder you're not married. Forget Bachelor of the Year, you could be Bachelor of the Millennium."

"Hey, I could get married if I wanted," he said. "I've had plenty of proposals."

"From living, breathing women with self-respect?"

His face darkened, so Gaby hurried on. "The bachelor contest is holding a reception at the track on Saturday night. The magazine's editor will be there, along with a bunch of readers who've won tickets to the event. You need to take an interest in every woman you talk to. I want the buzz to be about what an incredible guy you are, and how no one would ever have guessed it."

His eyes narrowed. "For someone whose job involves a lot of diplomacy, you can be pretty rude."

"You bring out the worst in me," she said apologetically.

"Do you always blame your clients for your bad behavior?"

"You're the first," she said. "It's curiously liberating."

Zack chuckled, and as always, the deep, warm sound shifted something at Gaby's core, unsettling her. She pressed her shoes into the carpet, seeking solid ground. "To prepare for Saturday night, we're going to do some role-playing," she said, "to polish up your conversation skills."

He groaned.

"You don't drive a NASCAR Sprint Cup Series race without practicing first, do you?"

"I guess not," he muttered.

"Okay, let's get started then." She stood up. "I'll be the magazine editor."

"Who should I be?" he deadpanned.

Goodness, was Zack Matheson making a joke? Gaby laughed, then sobered as she stuck out a hand. "Zack, nice to meet you. I'm Diana Vernay, editor of *Now Woman*."

"Great to meet you." Zack stood to shake hands. Gaby ignored the pulsing of electricity between them.

"I'm a big fan of your magazine," he said.

Gaby snickered.

Zack pressed his hand to his chest, wounded. "What?"

"I forgot to say, make it convincing. She won't believe you're a fan of *Now Woman* magazine. She'll know you're a kiss-up."

"You're a cynic," he accused her. "I'll have you know, their article on cuticle care had me on the edge of my seat."

Gaby found herself laughing again. "We agreed you'd take this training seriously," she reminded him. She had the sense that too much kidding around with Zack could be dangerous.

"Fine." He reached for her hand again.

Gaby whipped it behind her back. "Let's take the hand-shake as read." They had a lot of role-plays to get through. If she held his hand for each one, she'd be a mess.

His mouth twitched. "Okay, are you still the editor?"

"No, I'm one of the readers." She lifted her voice to a breathless squeak. "Wow, Zack, it's great to meet you. You're even handsomer in real life than you are on TV."

He just managed to catch an eye-roll. He smiled down at her. "You're too kind. But I'm kinda the ugly one in my family. My brothers are much better looking."

Nice. But Gaby wasn't about to let him off that easily. In the same persona, she simpered, "I have to admit, I'm a big fan of Trent's. He's the best driver on the track."

A sudden, heavy silence.

A muscle ticked in Zack's jaw. Then he smiled, albeit

grimly, and said, "I'll be sure and tell Trent you said that. Right after I beat him on Sunday."

His slow exhale told her the question had strained his good manners. She considered it a plus. She liked that flashing a smile he didn't mean or uttering an empty compliment didn't come easily. Zack thought deeply, cared deeply. If he ever opened up enough to fall in love with a woman, she'd know it was forever. Yikes, where did that come from?

"I—you—that was perfect," Gaby stuttered. He still looked tense, so she reached out to touch his hand. With the split-second reactions of a top NASCAR driver, he wrapped his fingers around hers. When she tried to pull away, he held fast.

"Y'know, there's something you could really help me out with," he said thoughtfully. "It's kind of embarrassing, but it's happened before, and I know it'll happen again."

Wow, he was actually asking for help? "What is it?" Her words came out breathless, thanks to the hand-holding thing they still had going on. Gaby tried to pretend they weren't touching each other, and gave him a bright, inquisitorial look.

"Sometimes when I go out in public," he said, his eyes on the view through the window of the park across the street, "women…accost me."

She just bet they did. But she let her brow wrinkle and said a surprised, "Really?"

He grinned. "Living, breathing women with self-respect," he assured her.

She narrowed her eyes. "That's the problem you want my help with? Women accosting you?"

"It can be hard to make it clear I'm not interested without causing offence," he said. "Presumably you don't want me offending people at the Bachelor of the Year event."

Was it her imagination, or was it getting hotter in here? Gaby lifted the weight of her hair off her neck. When Zack followed the movement with his eyes, she dropped her hands.

"What happens when you *are* interested in the woman?" she asked. "I guess the accosting's not a problem then."

"I can deal with that," he assured her. "I want help with the other kind."

"I guess I can give you some general pointers," she began.

"The role-play thing really helps," he said, an unholy glint in his eye.

Gaby tried staring him down, but he'd had years more practice at playing tough than she had.

"So, a role-play," he said. "Let's assume I'm not interested. And that you're a woman who is."

"Is what?" She stalled for time.

"Interested," he clarified.

She said slowly, "So, you want me to pretend to be interested in you, so you can practice rebuffing me politely."

"Bingo."

She slanted him a dark look. "And this isn't some kind of punishment for my forcing you to do charm school?"

He was all wide-eyed innocence. "I don't know what you mean."

She tried to look disapproving, but a smile kept tugging her mouth out of line. "Okay," she said, resigned. "I suppose it's conceivable this situation could come up on the weekend. Let's get started."

Zack folded his arms, watching her. And Gaby developed a massive case of stage fright. Something about *pretending* she was interested in Zack Matheson was deeply disturbing.

She cleared her throat. He smiled.

She ran her hands through her hair, mussing it. He straightened.

She took a couple of steps toward him, hips swinging. His gaze sharpened.

"Zack Matheson, it's so cool to meet you," she cooed. "I'm such a fan, you wouldn't believe."

His soft snort told her he *didn't* believe it—she dropped

out of character long enough to squint a warning at him. Then she twittered, "This is so amazing, seeing you here. I dreamed about you last night."

Zack's jolt told her he hadn't expected that. She hadn't intended to let it slip, either, but the dream was obviously at the forefront of her mind. Still, why not use what she had? The general gist, if not the details.

"What kind of dream?" He didn't sound nearly as nervous as he should if a strange woman came up and shared her dreams with him.

Time to up the ante. "You—you kissed me." The provocative fan comment Gaby intended came out a faltering mess. Zack froze. Had he guessed she'd just revealed her real dream? Did the fact that he wasn't talking mean he was horrified, or just plain embarrassed? Mortification heated Gaby's face. How could she look her client in the eye again? Just because they'd had the occasional moment of connection, it was totally inappropriate for her to—

She halted her panicked thoughts, aware of Zack's wary expression. She had to brazen this out, convince him the dream was all part of her act. She forced a saucy smile, put her hands on her hips and said in her pouting, stalker-fan persona, "Any chance you can make my dream come true?"

She expected him to get a hunted look, maybe even to bolt from the room. Then she would give him a stern lecture about how to handle unwanted attention and they would move into safer territory.

But nothing about today was going as she'd expected.

She gasped as his hands settled on her shoulders.

"Zack," Gaby cautioned in her normal voice. Then, when she caught the intensity, the silver sheen of desire in his eyes, the word faded away. She swallowed.

"Let's see if I can help with that dream," he said huskily.

He lowered his mouth to hers. *Pull away,* Gaby told herself. *Prove you're only playacting.*

Instead, she shifted closer to him. She'd expected his lips to be firm...but their warmth took her by surprise. So did the instant, consuming flare of longing. When she would have jolted back in shock, his hands anchored her.

Zack coaxed her with his mouth, cleverly used his tongue to part her lips, his hands to trace the length of her spine, the curve of her derriere. Gaby pressed herself closer to the lean hardness of his body and found the perfect complement for her own softness. He deepened the kiss, drawing an unfamiliar groan from her...one that he matched.

She had never known a sensation as sweet as this, Gaby thought dazedly. She couldn't get enough of Zack's mouth, of the glorious, male taste of him.

A voice in her head said, *If Sandra could see you now...*

What the heck was she doing? *Kissing my client.* With an almighty effort of will, Gaby twisted free. And immediately felt the loss of warmth. *Zack Matheson is not warm,* she reminded herself.

"That was terrible," she said, breathing unfortunately heavily.

He narrowed his eyes, folded his arms. "Terrible?"

"It's...it won't be clear to a woman who accosts you that you're not interested if you...if you grab her and kiss her." She tried to sound coolly professional, not easy when her insides were spinning doughnuts.

Zack threw back his head and laughed.

"Oh, yeah, now you grow a sense of humor," she said crossly, and he laughed harder.

"We both know that had nothing to do with a role-play," he said. "And everything to do with me wanting to kiss you, and—" his mouth curved in satisfaction "—you wanting it just as badly."

"That's not the point," she said. "Okay, so we had a momentary attraction. But the reason we're doing these role-plays is serious. It's about keeping your sponsor happy."

"It's about your promotion." His expression was unreadable.

"That, too," she said. If Sandra suspected for one second Gaby was being distracted by a man, let alone a client... "Zack, we need to agree on this—no more fooling around."

ONE PART OF ZACK'S BRAIN recognized that fooling around with Gaby was a bad idea. The other part, the bigger part, was totally hung up on how to get his lips back onto hers.

Kissing her had been incredible. And...fun. *Fun?* Not a word Zack applied much to his own life. But something about locking lips with Gaby, and locking wits over this stupid contest...he was having more fun than he'd had in years.

But he didn't race the NASCAR Sprint Cup Series for fun. Winning a race took focus and damn hard work. Serious business. So even though he suspected he never would have stopped kissing Gaby if she hadn't ended it herself, this thing needed to end right now.

"You're right," he said. "Fooling around does complicate things. It's not as if you and I could ever have a relationship."

Too late, Zack realized that was tactless. Gaby was right, he didn't think of others when he spoke.

"That's for sure," she said coolly. "My policy is to steer clear of self-centered men."

Ouch, he really had offended her. "I didn't mean I don't like you."

From her rising color, he guessed he was some way short of graduating charm school. He should shut up before he made things worse.

"Let's face it," Gaby said with a lightness Zack sensed wasn't genuine. "If we had a...relationship, next thing you know you'd convince me to give you an inch, and then you'd forget about the bachelor contest, forget about our deal, and never look up from that race car. And that would be the end of my promotion."

Her logic was impeccable, but suddenly Zack wasn't so sure. Because he'd been thinking about Gaby way more than he should. She had some kind of hold over him. That couldn't be good.

"Yeah, I'd do all that," he lied. "And even if I didn't, you're not my type." Shutting up would definitely have been a good idea. Her eyes widened with hurt. "You heard what I told the *Now Woman* reporter," he said roughly. "I want a woman who makes home and family—*my* home and family—her life."

She looked relieved to be reminded. "Like I said, you're self-centered."

It was funny how she was allowed to insult him with importunity, Zack thought, yet she got upset when he wasn't a hundred percent tactful in his response. Which again proved she was right—he had a lot to learn.

"I prefer to think of it as self-preservation." He'd been behind his brothers, no matter what he did, his whole life. It wasn't unreasonable to want a woman who put him first. Gaby would never be that woman—she'd admitted outright she wouldn't let a man get in the way of her career. And yet, that kiss…

Zack felt as if things were more complicated than he'd ever asked for them to be. As if he was getting himself tied up in knots. He had enough complications as it was.

"Let's get back to work," he said. "I have a flight to Watkins Glen to catch, and I wouldn't want to screw up this bachelor party for you."

CHAPTER NINE

AMBER'S TESTOSTERONE antennae were on full alert from the moment she pulled up outside the concrete-and-glass Matheson Racing building on Thursday morning. She gritted her teeth and cursed Brady Matheson.

She'd asked him to find her some work at Matheson Performance Industries, his engine-building company. Instead, he'd offered her a part-time receptionist job at the race team headquarters. Amber suspected he was trying to keep her away from her mom, who still worked as his secretary. More a second-in-command these days, was how Brady had put it. Which sounded as if he appreciated Julie-Anne…but Amber didn't trust large, charismatic men who tried to come between her and her mother.

Give him the benefit of the doubt, she admonished herself for the hundredth time. *Give everyone, everything, the benefit of the doubt.*

She locked her car and headed inside. The receptionist, a woman around Amber's age, smiled. "May I help you?"

"I'm Amber Blake. I'm, uh—" She indicated the reception desk.

The woman squealed. "You're the one who's going to fill in for me while I attend classes." She stood and shook Amber's hand. "I'm Libby. Am I ever pleased to see you."

"Have you been desperate to get away?" Amber asked. Good grief, she had to stop seeing monsters under every bed.

"Are you kidding?" Libby pushed a clipboard across the

counter and showed Amber where to sign in. "Chad practically forced me to enroll for my degree in motor sport management. Now that I'm about to start, I'm really looking forward to it, but I was starting to worry Chad would be answering the phones himself." She laughed.

Okay, a receptionist encouraged to enroll for a college degree obviously wasn't in need of rescue. Amber signed her name…then realized the pen had a fluffy pink pig stuck on the end. Libby was the woman with the stuffed animal fetish, as Trent had called it. She was to blame for that awful teddy bear Brady had bought.

"I'll let Chad know you're here," Libby said. "He wants to show you around." She picked up the phone.

To her left, Amber heard the click of a security lock. The receptionist looked past Amber, and dropped the phone back into its cradle. Her eyes brightened, her cheeks turned pink. "Hi, Ryan," she said.

"Hey, Libby, you look pretty today."

The voice was smooth, warm, beguiling—and it sent a tingle of warning down Amber's spine. She turned to look at the new arrival.

She had to lift her gaze, because the owner of the smooth voice was taller than average. Six feet, probably, with broad shoulders and narrow hips. Chocolate-brown eyes met hers, and immediately warmed to cinnamon.

"Hi," he said. How could one word sound so suggestive? Amber muttered a hello.

"Ryan, this is Amber Blake, Julie-Anne's daughter. She'll be working part-time on reception," Libby said. "Amber, Ryan Thorne is our NASCAR Nationwide Series driver."

"Nice to meet you, Amber," Ryan drawled. His gaze traveled over her, and it was evident from his smile that he liked what he saw. He stuck out a hand and seemed to notice at the same moment she did that he was holding a beer bottle.

Beer? At nine in the morning? Amber pulled her hand back swiftly.

Ryan laughed. "I forgot I had this." He waved the bottle at her. "We had a camera crew in just now, filming a commercial for my sponsor."

He tapped his chest, and she noticed his black T-shirt sported an orange-and-green Katzenberg Beer logo. "No other beer makes me feel this good," he said.

Why on earth did he think she wanted to know about his beer preferences? Or was he just totally self-obsessed? Ryan chuckled at her obvious bemusement. "That's my line from the commercial," he explained. "You wouldn't believe how many times I had to say it before I nailed it."

"Taking a swig of that—" she nodded at the near-empty bottle "—each time, I suppose."

He raised his eyebrows at the disapproval in her tone. "Libby, honey—" he winked at the receptionist "—can you dispose of this bottle for me? You know Dave won't allow alcohol in the workshop during working hours, not even in the trash."

"I'll take it to the recycling bin," Libby said with alacrity. Amber noticed that when she took the bottle, she held it exactly where Ryan's fingers had been.

"You're the best," he said lightly.

Blushing, Libby hurried out the back, with the promise she'd be only half a minute, which left Amber alone with Ryan. If he hadn't been obviously younger than she was, she might have felt threatened by such blatant male egotism. Instead, she took the opportunity to let off some of the steam she'd been holding in around her mom. "Something wrong with your legs, that you can't take out your own trash?" she asked.

He grinned. "I didn't want to deprive Libby of one of the high points of her day."

"Doing your bidding?" Amber said, disgusted.

"She has a passion for recycling," Ryan said, deadpan.

Amber scowled. Add twenty years, a beer belly and a foul

temper, and Ryan could pass for Billy Blake. He had all the "right" qualities: inappropriate consumption of alcohol, too aware of his own charms and not afraid to use them to manipulate people into doing what he wanted.

His smile widened in the face of her scowl. "It's been nice meeting you, Amber. I'm sure you'll be a real asset to Matheson Racing."

"I'm sure you will, too," she said. "When you grow up."

She held her breath, expecting to check off another of her dad's traits: an anger problem. But although Ryan's gaze didn't hold as much humor as before, he didn't exhibit any signs of a rage that might turn mean. He probably thought she was kidding. When he smiled slowly, she knew she was right.

"I look forward to getting to know you better," he drawled. He gave Amber a half salute and said, "Later."

She watched him disappear through the security door marked Workshop.

Not if I can help it, Amber thought. Giving this place the benefit of the doubt didn't have to include Ryan, did it? Because she was certain she had him pegged.

THE TRACK AT WATKINS GLEN was one of two road courses used in the NASCAR Sprint Cup Series. Zack loved the road courses, this one and the one at Sonoma, California. The Watkins Glen track was never straightforward, never predictable. Zack relished that complexity: it felt as if he was unraveling the race, rather than just driving it.

Midmorning on Saturday, he stepped out of the hauler and scanned the garage area for Gaby once again. He glanced at his watch—she should have been here by now. Unless she was still mad at him over his insensitivity the other day, but he didn't think that was likely.

The more Zack reflected on that kiss—which he did often—the more he was glad it had happened. If it hadn't, he and Gaby would still be on tenterhooks over their sizzling attraction. Now they'd brought it out into the open, and agreed it was a bad idea. Which meant they could now ignore it. They'd spent the rest of his day at charm school on role-plays and discussions that had covered just about every situation Zack might find himself in with his family, fans, or the media.

Now, he was keen to put his charming new persona to the test. He just needed Gaby here to remind him to think twice before he said something that might inflame his rivalry with Trent, or something that would push Chad's stress levels beyond the tipping point. She was helpful when his dad hassled him, too, as he'd discovered at dinner with Amber last week. A sympathetic, knowing look from Gaby had defused the situation, stopping Zack from taking offence when he knew, in his heart, Brady probably hadn't intended any.

They'd agreed that if things did turn sour with his brothers this weekend, Gaby would make some comment—put a spin on it, was the professional term—that would help the other guys see the problem in a different light. Another reason why Zack needed her here.

Finally he caught sight of her coming through the security check. He waited, taking in her figure in her blue-and-white check blouse and white jeans. On this hot day she looked cool. And tempting.

She spotted Zack, and beamed. His heart did an unexpected somersault. Then he realized Gaby was waving something at him…a magazine?

"Sorry I'm late, I had to wait for this to arrive before I could fly up," she called as she got closer. "It's a copy of *Now Woman,* hot off the press."

He'd forgotten all about the magazine profile. "How is it?"

She thrust the magazine into his hands. "They loved you." Beneath the headline—*Comeback Zack: Our Man of the Week*—Zack saw his own face looking out from the cover. He wasn't used to that. Trent was the cover model in this family.

Occasionally Chad made it to a cover, too. But the only place Zack was comfortable being "out there" was on the track.

The photo—huh, when had they taken that? His eyes were…soulful. Ugh. Sappy. He looked like a lost puppy, dammit, pleading *take me home*.

"They airbrushed this picture," he said, outraged. "No way did I look this pathetic."

"Are you kidding?" She grabbed the magazine back. "This photo is stunning. You look amazing. When this hits the stands next week, every woman in the U.S.A. is going to want you for her very own." Gaby stared down at the cover as if she wanted to take him home herself, and some of Zack's discomfort vanished.

"Amazing, huh?" he said.

"Yeah." She was still looking at the picture. Was it his imagination, or did her mouth soften? Damn, it had been so long since that kiss—two whole days. He needed to do it again, almost as badly as he needed to win a race.

Hell.

Zack slammed the brakes on that line of thought. He was getting way too serious.

She glanced up, caught him looking, and her cheeks pinkened. Muttering something about congratulating the journalist on a great story, she pulled out her cell phone and began scrolling through the numbers.

He reached a finger and touched her cheek. Her head whipped around. "What was that for?"

"Instinct." As in, he couldn't resist.

"Don't act on your instincts," she ordered, then blushed deeper.

Zack chuckled. "Come into the hauler, we'll celebrate the article with a soda."

Inside, they both reached for the door of the chiller cabinet at the same time; their fingers brushed.

"Will you stop that?" she snapped.

"If I wanted to get my hands on you," he said, "I wouldn't resort to sneaky touches."

She frowned. "Are you saying you don't want to get your hands on me?"

He'd offended her again? He cursed, and Gaby laughed as she flipped the tab on her soda. "You're really not very good at this, are you?" she said. "Even after all our hard work."

"Depends what you're talking about." Zack ran his thumb across the seam of her lips…which had the gratifying result of softening them, parting them. The pink tip of Gaby's tongue emerged, flicked against Zack's thumb.

"Make yourselves comfortable, you two," an amused voice said from behind Zack.

Hell. Zack turned, slowly to show he wasn't embarrassed. "Butt out, Trent," he said, more relaxed than he felt.

Trent chuckled.

Gaby wasn't quite so relaxed. Her color turned beet-red, and she chugged back her drink as if she'd just wandered in out of a desert.

"Ready for practice?" Zack asked Trent.

Trent nodded. "Sure." He helped himself to a soda. "I like the Glen. Not many people I can't beat here."

"You might have to work for it tomorrow." Zack had qualified sixth yesterday, one of his better qualifying laps this year. And for once, better than Trent, who would start the race in tenth position.

"I'm not worried," Trent said. Zack knew it was true, his little brother always had a surfeit of confidence. "I figure you benefited from the warmer track surface yesterday, qualifying later in the day than I did," Trent continued.

"You don't think I just drove better than you?" Zack suggested.

"No way." Trent smirked.

Zack caught Gaby's eye. She made a winding motion with her hand, and, far from losing his temper, Zack found himself struggling not to laugh at his brother's blatant attempt to undermine his confidence.

"You're absolutely right," he told Trent. "When we get into that race, chances are you'll pass me before our first pit stop."

"Damn right." Trent snickered…then it clicked that he hadn't gotten the response he'd expected. Suspicious, he said, "Whaddya mean?"

"Just what I said." Zack grinned.

"You're seriously saying I'm going to pass you early on, and stay that way."

Zack shrugged. "History suggests it."

Trent shoved his hands in his pockets. "What are you playing at?"

Zack patted his brother on the shoulder, pretending a superiority he seldom felt with his younger sibling. "Good luck out there, man."

Trent practically ran out of the hauler. Zack would bet money he was off to find Kelly and get some psychological analysis of what just happened. Didn't matter. What mattered was that Zack had resisted falling into a negative behavior pattern that would keep the rift growing between him and his family.

"You did great," Gaby said.

"Thanks." Zack looked down at her face—that fair skin, her raspberry-pink mouth—and felt a pang of regret because despite the little game they'd just been playing, he couldn't kiss her.

CHAPTER TEN

SUNDAY, RACE DAY, WAS fine and clear, beating the weather forecasters' prediction of showers. Zack took it as a good sign, but he knew forty-two other drivers would be doing the same. He couldn't put his confidence in signs and superstitions—he had to get out on the track and build on his sixth-place start. Without losing the plot, or control of his car.

Gaby had somehow convinced a motorsports correspondent from a New York paper to talk to Zack. They'd had a brief interview that Zack thought went all right. "Maybe a little bland," he suggested to Gaby as they crossed from the media center to the garage.

"Bland is good if the alternative is you losing your cool," she said. "But, yeah, you could afford to be a little more quotable."

"Maybe something along the lines of 'mistakes I've made at Watkins Glen'?"

"That works," she said. The vibe between them was companionable, easy.

Zack registered a shriek in the distance, but it wasn't until they were nearer the garage that he realized a posse of young women were screaming his name.

"It *is* him," a tall blonde wearing microscopic cutoffs said. "I told you."

"Zack!" A curly-haired brunette waved. "You can be butter in my hands anytime."

"That's what you told *Now Woman* about your dad and Julie-Anne," Gaby murmured.

"You said it wasn't out until next week."

"I think electronic subscribers get it early."

The women reached them. "We saw you in *Now Woman*," one of them said breathlessly.

"Great," Zack said. He'd skimmed the article, and no way did the softhearted, mushy guy it talked about bear any resemblance to him. Not to mention the guy in the article apparently had chiseled cheekbones. What the hell were chiseled cheekbones? They sounded damn painful.

He glanced around for an escape route.

"You need to talk to them," Gaby said. "I know you want to get to the garage and get your mind into race mode, but the bachelor contest…"

He'd promised, so he would do it. "I'm glad you enjoyed the magazine," he said.

The brunette giggled. "I love your voice."

He was aware of Gaby shifting at his side. But he wasn't worried, they'd practiced how he would fend off unwanted advances.

"I don't sound quite so relaxed when my spotter tells me there's a pileup in front of me," he said.

Cue more giggling, all around.

"So, do you ever, like, date your fans?" the tall blonde asked.

"Not all at once," Zack joked. Then realized he'd gotten overconfident, and accidentally implied he would date a fan. Which he supposed he would, if he met someone he liked, but he seldom talked to a fan long enough to get that far. The women in front of him now wore varying shades of hopeful.

"Look at you all," he said. "You're all gorgeous. Any man would be lucky to have you."

Someone sighed.

"But I usually have to know a woman pretty well before I ask her for a date," he said. "It's important to be friends first."

Several women looked disappointed, but one murmured to her friend, "He's deep."

Huh, that was what Gaby had said. He had hidden depths. Zack had thought it a euphemism for "lacks charm."

"If you want to get to know me before you ask me on a date…" The tall blonde pulled a crumpled receipt from her pocket—extracting it from such tight pants was an act of eye-watering contortion—and scribbled on the back. "Here's my number."

Zack took it. He had to be polite, right? Three other women handed him their numbers. One was clearly a professional groupie; her card had her photo and *I heart NASCAR* on it.

"Can I give you a kiss for luck?" the curly-haired brunette—Susannah, if he'd read her card right—asked.

Gaby grabbed Zack's arm. "So sorry, ladies, but if Zack doesn't leave now he'll be late for the driver's briefing, and you all know what that means."

Wincing and eye-widening suggested they understood that if Zack was late by even one second to the driver's meeting he'd have to start the race off at the back of the field, which would be particularly painful given how well he'd qualified.

The women instantly relinquished all claim on him.

"Just be sure and text your votes for Zack into the bachelor contest," Gaby said over her shoulder as she hustled him toward the garage area. A chorus of promises of multiple votes followed them.

"I thought I handled that pretty well," Zack said

"You were fine." She put on a spurt of speed.

"I was good," he insisted.

"Do you want me to get rid of those phone numbers for you?" Her gaze was fixed on their destination. Only her unusual speed alerted Zack to her tension.

"Sure," he said.

She slowed. "You don't want to call any of those women?"

"Nope."

"Not even the blonde? She was hot."

He gave her a measuring look. "You heard me, I like to get to know someone before I ask them on a date."

"Uh-huh."

"Are you jealous?" he asked.

"Of course not." She tossed her head, and her hair swung behind her.

They'd reached the garage area, and Zack found himself the target of more female fans clustered there. It appeared every woman at the track was an online subscriber to *Now Woman.* By the time he'd forced his way through the crowd without offending anyone, he was dangerously close to tardy.

He left Gaby, sprinted to the meeting and made it just in time. As he sank into the plastic seat, he realized he was still clutching a wodge of phone numbers.

THE GREEN FLAG FELL, and Zack put everything out of his mind that wasn't to do with the feel of the car, the grip of the track, the need to turn, to pass, to run faster and better than everyone else.

His spotter, Mac, called in a smash on the second lap, and Zack managed to avoid it. When the green flag came back out, he was in fourth place. Way too early to get excited—he still had hours to run—but something thrilled inside him.

"Where's Trent?" he couldn't help but ask his team when he pulled in for his first pit stop. They barely had time to answer him, but the guy replacing Zack's right front tire said, "Twelve."

Huh, Trent had fallen back. No denying that did something for Zack's confidence. He had the craziest urge to hum as he got back on the track from pit road. He laughed at himself.

"What's so funny?" his crew chief growled through the earpiece.

"It's a beautiful day," Zack said.

"Uh, Zack…" Chad now. "You okay?"

"Dandy," he said, as he swept past Danny Cruise, and caught a one-fingered salute for his efforts.

"Nice move," Chad said. Then he evidently decided to shut up and leave Zack to it—to what became one of those races a driver doesn't get very often, where he can do no wrong, where obstacles melt away, or are navigated with no more difficulty than a pile of sludge after a spring thaw.

Zack swept over the finish line on a wave of speed and glory. He'd won!

The crowd went wild as he drove his victory lap. Trent had a habit of spinning doughnuts all the way around the track in this situation. Zack contented himself with one doughnut as he returned to the finish line, then he headed for Victory Lane and his team.

Already he knew how he wanted to celebrate tonight. He would invite Gaby out for dinner.

GABY COULDN'T STOP GRINNING, no matter that she was supposed to be a seasoned PR operative, surprised at nothing. Every minute of Zack's race had been sheer joy.

"Did you see that? Did you see Zack?" she babbled to one of the industry's most hardened reporters.

"I did," he said dryly.

Gaby tried to reclaim some professional distance. "I daresay you'll want to interview him."

His chuckle told her she wasn't fooling anyone. Mentally, she ran through a list of the people her client should talk to once he was done with the shouted questions and quick photos here in Victory Lane. Today, they could pick and choose.

She could get some serious mileage out of this for the bachelor contest, too. *Man of the Week is Man of the Day,* that kind of thing. Gaby pulled out her cell and called Leah Gibbs, the junior account exec who acted as Motor Media Group's gofer at the track on race days.

She allocated Leah some of Zack's free time over the next day or two, and asked her to set up some of the appointments. Gaby would call Diana at *Now Woman* herself.

As she talked to the editor, Zack caught her eye across the throng. He grinned, and she gave him the thumbs-up.

By the time Zack left Victory Lane, she could see his adrenaline levels were dropping, exhaustion was kicking in. Though he still had a spring in his step, his shoulders drooped slightly.

"You need an early night," she said. She knew he didn't plan to head back to Charlotte until tomorrow.

"Funny you should mention that," he said. "I was about to ask you to a celebration dinner."

"Who else is going?"

"No one."

Her stomach flipped. "You mean, like a date?"

"Yeah, very like a date."

The knowledge that he wanted to be with her above everyone else made her tempted, seriously tempted. But while Sandra didn't forbid her staff to date clients, she'd made it clear she didn't think Gaby could keep her priorities straight if she was dating. "Remember what we agreed? We wouldn't suit each other—you're too selfish, I'm too ambitious."

"In which case it would hardly be fair to inflict ourselves on other people," he said reasonably. "We deserve each other."

Gaby smiled. "I'm sure one of those girls who gave you their number today would make the sacrifice." Those girls were another excellent reason to refuse dinner. Every muscle in her body had tensed, she'd been rigid with jealousy, when they'd come after Zack. She'd wanted to smack them. She had no desire to be in such thrall to any man, least of all one like Zack, who would never return the favor.

He fished in his pocket, held something out to her. Gaby took it…and realized it was a crumpled bundle of phone numbers.

"I think I mentioned, I prefer to date women I already like," Zack said.

He was making it hard. But Gaby still had a modicum of strength. She curled her fingers around the tattered phone numbers.

"Zack, I won't go to dinner with you," she said. "Go with your family, they should be the ones to share this moment with you."

He'd talked to her once about self-preservation. That was what she had to practice now. Before she did something stupid, like lose her heart.

AMBER SHIVERED AS SHE stepped out the door of Matheson Racing into a morning made cool by an unseasonable wind. She could feel the flesh on her legs turning to goose bumps below her running shorts. She rubbed her arms briskly, and began to do her warm-ups. At seven-thirty on a Monday morning, there was no one to see her—the parking lot was vacant, except for one lone sports car over on the left that had obviously been there all night. Amber figured she could enjoy some peace and solitude on a one-hour jog, then shower and dress for work and be behind the reception desk at nine.

Not many staff came in on Mondays. Later, the tourists would arrive to visit the team store, but for now, the business park was near empty and it was easy to ignore the buildings in favor of the trees and grassy lawns.

She held on to her right foot, stretching her quad, then switched sides. Next she put one hand behind her neck, and clasped the elbow with her other hand. She repeated the exercise with the other arm, then dropped down into a lunge.

The slam of a car door turned her attention to the lone sports car that had been parked all night.

Ryan Thorne was crossing the pavement and coming toward her.

"Hey," he called.

Amber wobbled in her lunge. "Hi," she said discouragingly.

But he was one of those guys who never took a hint. Insensitive, interested only in what he wanted. He was smiling as he reached the steps and looked up at her. Amber fought the urge to tug her tank top down. Her goose bumps grew more pronounced.

"I didn't see you at the Glen," he said.

"I wasn't there." Her mom and Brady had invited her to fly to the race on their plane. Amber had acted suitably grateful, but she'd refused. She had so many bad memories of race tracks, of her father losing it under pressure, of the blazing arguments after they arrived home, she had no interest. However, she knew Zack had won his race, and Ryan had trailed the field in the NASCAR Nationwide Series race, which wasn't uncommon recently.

Ryan wore snug-fitting jeans with a black T-shirt that molded to his biceps and offset his sandy blond hair. As he walked up the steps, Amber was irritated to feel a frisson of awareness. *Yeah, yeah, good-looking guy, big deal,* she told her hormones.

"Are you going to Patsy Grosso's birthday party on Wednesday?" he asked.

"I doubt it." She folded her arms across her chest, trying to imply her life was none of his business without actually saying so.

As he came close, she absorbed the fact that his rumpled hair wasn't the designer kind of rumpling, and he needed a shave. Plus, he smelled. It was the warm, earthy smell of a guy who'd just woken up. Something primitive tugged in Amber's stomach. "Did you sleep in your car?"

He rubbed his stubbled jaw. "Yeah."

"Too drunk to drive home?" Her father had often claimed to have slept in his car. It had taken Julie-Anne a long time to see what was obvious to Amber—that her dad was spending his nights with other women.

He scowled. "I wasn't drunk. I had an argument with my father and needed to get out of the house. I planned to sleep on the couch in reception, but I forgot my card-key."

"You still live with your parents?" He was twenty-six years old, according to Libby, her fellow receptionist. "Can't you look after yourself?"

RYAN COULDN'T FIGURE OUT why this woman had such a downer on him. He'd spoken to her maybe a dozen times since she started working for the team, and he was yet to receive a smile. Which was especially annoying because he'd seen her smile, at her mom, at Chad and Zack, and he wanted that smile for himself.

He couldn't engage her in a discussion of the races—he'd tried, but gotten nowhere. She didn't attend them and he had a suspicion she didn't even watch them on TV, which for a woman with her NASCAR background was bizarre.

Or maybe she did watch the races, but she just didn't like Ryan. Again, he struggled to understand. Sure, he'd been known to tick women off by ending it when they got too serious, but he hadn't asked Amber out yet, and she was already acting as if he'd dumped her.

It wasn't fair, he thought. Especially when she was so damn pretty that he'd thought about dating her the moment they'd met. She had an amazing figure, slim in the right places, and curvy in the best places. And her dark hair and olive-toned skin made her seem exotic.

She thought he was a mama's boy, going by that dig she'd just made.

"I've looked after myself for years," he said. "I moved back in with my folks when Matheson Racing hired me. Dad pointed out that I wouldn't want to be worrying about an apartment while on the road constantly."

His father had omitted to mention that the right to question Ryan's every move was part of the bargain. That was the cause of last night's argument and many others previously.

Maybe that was why he was so drawn to Amber. Everything about her shrieked independence and a determination not to do things just because someone else wanted her to.

"How about I take you out to dinner tonight?" he said.

She straightened up. "Excuse me?"

"I'll take you to BamBam," he offered generously. "It's the

coolest place in Charlotte." He usually took first dates somewhere less expensive, but he figured nothing less than his best effort would work on Amber.

"No thanks."

Ryan tried to think of the last time a girl had turned him down for a date, and failed to recall such an incident. Amber clearly had no compulsion to explain her refusal. Strangely, he liked that. *I'm a masochist, wanting only what I can't have.* Which pretty much summed up his racing at the moment.

"Is it the age difference?" he asked. "Because I can handle an older woman."

"Don't even think about handling me," she warned.

"How old are you, anyway?" he asked.

"Way, way too old for you."

"Your mom doesn't look that old, did she have you when she was twelve?"

She pffed, but her lips twitched.

"I saw that," he said. "You nearly smiled."

She rolled her eyes, but there was no animosity in it.

"Have dinner with me," he coaxed her. "The food will be great and you can ignore the company."

Again that twitch of the lips. She drew in a breath and Ryan thought *yes*. He was shocked how excited he was at the prospect of an evening with Amber.

"It's *very* nice of you to offer." She sounded as if she was appeasing a kindergartner. "But I don't date race car drivers."

"Why not?" The indignation in his voice definitely had a kindergarten quality. But he'd never heard anything so unreasonable.

"They're too slick," she said. "You can't trust a slick guy."

"Slick? That's not true," Ryan protested. "Look at Zack Matheson. Look at his dad—Brady used to drive, and no one would say he's slick."

"I don't trust the gruff type, either."

"Which camp have you pegged me for, slick or gruff?" They both knew he had to be at the slick end of her weird scale. It was a direct insult to his trustworthiness. He decided not to call her on it, not while there was still a chance he might get this date.

"Will you go out with me if I promise not to talk about NASCAR? We could pretend I'm a—a jockey." When her eyes flicked to his full six feet of height, he figured he'd snagged her interest.

She shook her head. "You can't not talk about NASCAR. You live for the sport."

He raised his hands in surrender. "Okay, what if it wasn't me? What about a stunningly good-looking driver from another team who can't speak due to a throat operation, and therefore physically can't talk about NASCAR? A guy who's not slick or gruff, and who's incredibly kind to children and animals."

She blinked at the convoluted scenario. "Nope."

"What if a driver saved your life, then he asked you on a date. Would you go out of gratitude?"

She laughed.

Her laugh was everything Ryan had anticipated, and more. Light, musical, clear in the morning air. It turned her eyes the sparkling blue of a spring sky, widened her mouth in a generous curve. He was bewitched.

"Maybe I'd go on one date out of gratitude," she conceded. "But that's all."

Ryan looked around, half hoping some nutcase would come speeding through the parking lot and up the steps so he could drag Amber to safety.

"Goodbye, Ryan." Before he could protest—and before he remembered to borrow her card-key—she burst the fantasy bubble and jogged down the steps, breaking into a run as she reached the bottom. She ran fast, as if she was trying to get away from something—him.

Okay, maybe their dinner date wouldn't happen tonight, Ryan thought, as he sat down on the steps to wait for another early bird. But it would happen.

CHAPTER ELEVEN

"YOU JOB IS TO BOOST my image," Zack said, as he thumbed the elevator button at the Charlotte Getaway Hotel. "So how come when I win a race, which is the best thing I can do for my image, you disappear?"

He sounded ticked off, and that's because he was. Right after Gaby had refused to go to dinner with him, she'd disappeared off somewhere and left him with her junior sidekick.

"Leah is very capable, she was following my instructions. I understand from her you did a great job in your interviews." Gaby stepped into the elevator.

"*You* are my PR rep," Zack persisted.

"And I was busy representing you." She glanced anxiously at her reflection in the polished steel doors. Zack could have told her she looked fantastic in her cream suit and her black silk blouse with large cream polka dots. "While you were doing those interviews, I was briefing *Now Woman* magazine and trying to convince the news desk at one of the major networks to interview you in their weekly roundup next Friday." Gaby paused. "How was your celebration dinner with your family?"

"It was fine," he admitted. "No one said anything stupid, mainly thanks to Kelly cracking the whip."

"Good." Gaby touched his arm, and for a second he couldn't move.

"You were right about me spending the evening with them," he said reluctantly. Reluctant because he still wanted to have that dinner date with her.

They reached the business center where Rob Hudson had arranged a meeting between his staff at Getaway and Matheson Racing, to talk about how they could build on Zack's win at Watkins Glen and the cover story in *Now Woman*.

When the meeting started, eight of them sat around the boardroom table: Zack, Chad and Steve Parr, Matheson Racing's day-to-day sponsor liaison for the No. 548 car; Gaby and Sandra from Motor Media Group; plus three guys from Getaway.

Zack was thankful that for once they were going into a meeting with a positive tone. The downside was, they wanted to set the PR strategy for the next four weeks leading up to the Chase for the NASCAR Sprint Cup. Zack wanted to set his racing strategy.

Gaby sent him a significant look and a teeth-gritted smile. Oh, yeah, he was supposed to smile. Zack followed orders, and her smile turned genuine. There was a lot a guy might do for a smile like that, he mused, as the meeting delved into media impressions and weightings. Zack listened with half an ear, and gathered that even without the win and the magazine profile his impressions had been more favorable over the past couple of weeks. But he still had some way to go before his name and face had the pulling power of, say, Trent.

He reined in his impatience as a marketing assistant from Getaway ran through a PowerPoint presentation. He could have told these people all of that without recourse to fancy charts, statistics and opinion surveys.

He preferred to watch Gaby—a far more pleasant occupation. She was angled toward Sandra as she watched the presentation. She looked just like the others—smart, capable, professional. Which was just as well, because these guys didn't pull their punches. The Getaway people had no qualms about complaining loud and long over any failure to meet expectations.

Twelve million dollars gave them that right, Zack supposed. The discussion moved on to the bachelor contest.

"*Now Woman* plans to run another story about Zack next week," Gaby said. Approving noises came from around the table.

"The first article was a great success. In the last week, our call center has taken a number of calls from people wanting to reserve a room Zack has slept in," Rob Hudson said. "I have to admit, I know the rest of my team liked the idea immediately, but I wasn't so sure about putting our focus on the contest when you had first mentioned it."

Huh, she hadn't told Zack that.

"Your own research shows women are the major vacation decision-makers," she said modestly.

"If Zack wins the bachelor contest—" Hudson addressed the assembled group "—we might have a hope of a decent return on the money Uncle Brian poured into this sponsorship." Uncle Brian was Brianna's late father. Just about the last thing he'd done before cancer struck him down was get board approval for a NASCAR Sprint Cup Series sponsorship. Rob turned to Gaby. "How do we make sure Zack wins?"

Sandra straightened in her seat and shot Gaby a loaded look.

"Winning the contest isn't something I can guarantee," Gaby began.

When Rob made an impatient movement, Zack saw something flash in Gaby's eyes. Something he recognized. Panic. The sense that although she was doing well, she was only hanging on by her fingernails, and that at any second now she would let go, hit the wall and screw up any one of a thousand ways that would cost her control of her future.

"Motor Media Group will do everything possible to advance Zack's cause," Sandra said. Which meant Gaby would do everything possible.

"I don't mind telling you, this NASCAR sponsorship has been a big disappointment to date," Rob said.

Gaby looked…besieged. Her demeanor reminded Zack of their first meeting, when she'd clearly been out of her depth, yet somehow, she'd pulled out her show-stopping accusation that he was a has-been, and he'd ended up agreeing to work with her.

Do it again, he advised her silently. *Find that sucker punch.*

But instead, he could see her going under, floundering as Rob Hudson suggested Getaway should pay on results, not effort. Sandra wasn't jumping in to help as she normally would—Zack guessed she saw this as some kind of test for Gaby. He frowned.

Chad noticed. "Zack, did you have something to add?"

Zack ditched the frown, in case anyone thought he was sponsor-hostile. While he had their attention he might as well say something to support Gaby. Right now she had no one else in her corner.

"Gaby has invested considerable time in preparing me for the bachelor contest," he said. "To be honest, she didn't get a lot of cooperation. But I've been pleasantly surprised at the outcome, and from now on I plan to put more effort in at my end."

Gaby's jaw dropped.

Hudson stared, as if Zack was speaking a foreign language.

Surely he hadn't been *that* uncooperative in previous meetings? Zack thought about how the relationship with Getaway had deteriorated since he'd won at Daytona, right before they'd signed the sponsorship deal, and realized he probably had.

"Excellent news," Sandra said, almost concealing her surprise.

Okay, babe, over to you, he telegraphed to Gaby.

Eyes shining, she grabbed the opportunity with both hands. "We've done extremely well with, as Zack said, less than his full endorsement of our program. Although we can't guarantee a win in the contest, we can guarantee an improved focus on media opportunities, and in my experience that always gets results."

Chad's smile was faintly ironic, but there was genuine warmth in his eyes as he looked at Zack—Zack knew he had Gaby to thank for that. Too late, Zack realized he'd probably just committed himself to a bunch of PR activities that weren't about racing. Yet the idea didn't worry him as much as he'd expected—obviously he was still riding a wave of confidence after his win, but could it last?

We'll make it last.

With a jolt, he realized the *we* included him and Gaby. Well, why the heck not? He and Gaby made quite a team.

PATSY GROSSO, OWNER, WITH her husband Dean, of Cargill-Grosso Racing, was one of NASCAR's best-known and most liked figures. So when the Grossos invited people to Patsy's fiftieth birthday party, held at a motorsports museum in Charlotte, around three hundred guests flocked to attend.

Gaby changed into her short, pale gray silk dress at the office, and traveled to the party with two of her colleagues. She looked her best. She'd put in an hour with her hair straightener in the office bathroom, and the beading around the scooped neckline made her figure-hugging dress even more elegant.

When they arrived at the museum, Gaby scanned the room, looking for Zack. She owed him her thanks for rescuing her from that awkward situation during Tuesday's meeting. She'd have sworn he'd been too focused on himself to observe her increasing desperation. But he'd shifted Getaway's, and more importantly Sandra's, perception in Gaby's favor.

She helped herself to a smoked salmon hors d'oeuvre from a tray proffered by a waiter whose white shirt bore the Gourmet by Grace logo.

Grace Winters, a celebrated chef from a family better known for producing top NASCAR crew chiefs, must have catered tonight's party, which meant the food would be wonderful. It was obvious no expense had been spared in creating the perfect occasion, as evidenced by the well-known jazz quartet playing at the far end of the room, and the lavish decorations. Swathes of gold silk formed a canopy that disguised the venue's exposed air-conditioning ducts, while black-and-white checkered ribbon streamed everywhere.

Given the number of people filling the room, it was odd that Gaby immediately spotted Zack amongst the crowd.

She caught her breath. In his dark shirt and dark pants, he was the best-looking man there. He glanced her way. Holding her gaze, Zack walked toward her.

He kissed her cheek—too fleeting. "You look great," he said.

Was it her imagination, or did he sound slightly husky?

The glint in his eye turned proprietary. "You'd better stick with me tonight," he said. "There's every chance I'll blow my new nice-guy image if you're not around."

She sighed. "A PR rep's work is never done."

He grinned, and that crooked grin tugged at her heart.

"Hey, you two." Chad approached, his arm around Brianna's waist. She looked so happy, content—as if she was in the best place in the world.

Gaby knew a sudden certainty that wrapped in Zack's arms would be an even better place.

Brianna was talking about tonight's festivities. She'd come to know Patsy well over the past few months, and had been involved in planning the party.

Gaby grabbed the reprieve from her thoughts of Zack, and threw herself into the safe conversation. "Everything seems to be going very smoothly," she said.

Brianna grimaced. "Grace is worried that she's shorthanded."

"She called Tony this afternoon and insisted he haul his butt here to help," Chad said.

"Tony?" Gaby asked, not caring in the least.

"Our team accountant, Tony Winters, is Grace's brother-in-law," Zack explained. "He owns part of the catering business with her, but he's usually hands-off."

"Interesting," Gaby said. And it was—when Zack's deep voice was doing the talking. The realization shook her.

"There he is now. He had to break a hot date to get here." Chad raised his voice to a good-looking, dark-haired man. "Hey, Tony, the uniform suits you." Chad grinned as his wife swatted his arm. Tony looked less than thrilled at the compliment—he gave Chad a tight smile and moved on.

By the time Gaby had displayed immense and entirely phony interest in Tony Winters's love life, Grace Winters's catering business and the party planning, she'd just about reined in her unhealthy awareness of Zack. When Sandra and Taney joined their circle, she dismissed Zack entirely from her thoughts. Sandra was too astute—she'd pick up on any vibe between Gaby and her client faster than a NASCAR Sprint Cup car could pass a checkered flag.

When Sandra touched her arm and indicated Gaby should step back from the group, her heart sank.

"I know this is a social occasion, not work," Sandra said. "But I'd like a word."

"Sure." Gaby rehearsed an argument to convince her boss she wasn't involved with Zack, her priorities were exactly where they should be.

Sandra drew her out of earshot. "I'm impressed by your work with Zack," she said. "You've surprised me, Gaby, in a good way. I didn't think you had it in you."

"To be honest, I wasn't sure, either," Gaby surprised herself by saying. "I hoped I did, but working with Zack…"

"It's pushed you to discover the extent of your abilities," Sandra said. "And it's clear to everyone now that those are considerable."

"Thank you," Gaby murmured, embarrassed by such lavish praise. It wasn't so much that she'd discovered new abilities, she thought, as it was that working with Zack had built her confidence, strengthened her, so her strengths and abilities could shine.

"Hey, I didn't hesitate to tell you when your work wasn't up to scratch," Sandra teased. "It's only fair that I tell you when the situation has changed."

Gaby caught her breath. "The situation?"

Sandra nodded, smiling. "I'm putting you back on the shortlist to stand in for me while I'm on maternity leave."

Gaby's heart raced. "That's wonderful."

"You earned it," Sandra said simply.

As she accepted Sandra's kiss on the cheek, Gaby saw Zack watching her. She couldn't hold in her delight as she smiled at him. He smiled back, and it seemed to her that the warmth beaming from him was hers alone.

ZACK COULDN'T BELIEVE HOW drawn he was to Gaby tonight. She still had that hint of vulnerability he'd seen in their meeting yesterday. Combine that with her outward confidence and her phenomenal beauty in that silky dress... From the moment she walked in, he'd wanted to kiss her again.

She and Sandra rejoined the group, which had swelled to include Amber, Trey Sanford and a couple other people. The conversation turned to speculation about who would make the Chase for the NASCAR Sprint Cup.

"Are you going to make it, Zack?" Amber asked.

It wasn't a topic Zack wanted to tempt fate by discussing. He shrugged and managed a tight smile at Amber. He wasn't sure what he thought of his new stepsister yet. Brady was bending over backward to make her feel welcome, and Zack had to admit that kind of stuck in his craw.

He told himself that wasn't Amber's fault. Then he put her out of his mind as Gaby made her way around to him. She leaned into him, and Zack caught the scent of roses and jasmine. "Sandra just put me back on the shortlist for the promotion," she said.

"That's fantastic," he said, thrilled for her. "*You're* fantastic."

She radiated suppressed excitement. "You get some of the credit, helping me out in that meeting yesterday."

"That was just one moment. It's taken a lot more than that to bring Sandra around." He didn't want to talk about work, he wanted to kiss her.

Chad and Brady edged into their conversation. "What are you and Gaby whispering about?" Chad asked.

"Nothing to do with you." Zack winked at Gaby.

"Did you ever meet a guy as secretive as Zack?" Chad demanded of his father. Zack froze—it wasn't the first time he'd been called secretive, usually as a prelude to a family argument.

"Never," Brady said solemnly.

Chad cuffed Zack on the shoulder. "Hey, man, the words you whisper to a beautiful woman are none of your family's business!" He grinned.

Relief flooded Zack. "At last, he gets it," he said to Gaby with exaggerated patience. She laughed, eyes dancing. He wanted to hold her.

"I need to whisper more words to this beautiful woman," he told Chad. Then, to Gaby, "Let's dance."

He half expected an argument, but instead she stepped into his arms.

The incredible rightness of the sensation floored Zack. No way, he told himself, could dancing with Gaby feel this…significant. Not after all they'd agreed on about how wrong they were for each other. *Tell that to my libido.* The band was playing a slow sad song. He tugged her closer, bent his head.

"No way," she said.

"What?"

"Don't even think about kissing me with your brother looking on and my boss hanging around."

"We'll go somewhere else, then." Ignoring her protest, he picked up the pace so they were wildly out of time with the music. He steered her through the darkened doorway of an anteroom. In the faint light that reached it from the main room, he could see an exhibition of sponsor logos from over the decades. "Just your kind of thing," he said, indicating the walls.

He pulled her farther into the room, where they couldn't be seen, and left the light off. No one would know they were here.

"What an incredible night," she said, sounding breathless and excited.

"Motor racing history really does it for me, too," he said.

Gaby giggled, a carefree sound he hadn't heard from her before. "You know what I mean," she said. "Sandra saying I'm up for the promotion, your dad and Chad kidding around with you like you're part of the family…"

"I know what you mean," he agreed.

"It looks," she said wonderingly, "as if we might both get what we want."

"Incredible," he said huskily, no longer talking about his family or her job. Gaby rose up on tiptoe to meet him; his mouth joined with hers. *This* was what he wanted. Needed.

Zack roamed her mouth. The darkness provided an immediate, added excitement, forcing him to rely on feel. On the sensation of her lips parted beneath his, seeking and giving. On the delighted, shivery response of her body to his touch. On the small sounds of need that escaped her, echoing Zack's own soft groan. Gaby was passionate and beautiful and responsive.

"This is such a bad idea," she murmured against his mouth.

"I can be bad if you can."

A stifled giggle. "That's not what I meant."

"Trust me, honey, this is a great idea." He took her mouth again, ran his hands over her, felt the warmth of her body through the thin silk. She stumbled in her high-heeled shoes, and kicked them off. Zack's lips found the column of her throat.

"Ouch," Gaby yelped.

Instantly, he lifted his head. "What'd I do?"

"It wasn't you, I stood on something sharp." She hopped slightly. "Yow, ow."

"Okay, honey, let's take a look." Zack fumbled for the light switch.

When the ancient fluorescent lighting flickered into action, Zack registered that Gaby looked delightfully disheveled. He bent to examine her foot.

"It's not a cut," she said. "I don't know what—"

"It was this." Zack picked up a cuff link off the floor. No ordinary cuff link, it comprised an enormous diamond encased in gold. Even Zack, who knew nothing about gems, could see it must be worth a fortune.

"Here's another one." Gaby bent down and picked up a matching cuff link that had ended up beneath a display case, probably scuffed there as Zack and Gaby kissed. This one was half-wrapped in a twist of tissue. Gaby handed it to Zack.

"I've seen these before, I can't think who they belong to." Zack wondered if one of the other guests had put the anteroom to the same use he and Gaby just had, and the cuff links had been pulled off in the heat of passion. He turned one of the links over and held it up to the light so he could read the engraving.

A shock ran through him; quickly, he flipped over the other link. "What the hell?"

"Is there a problem?" Gaby asked.

He passed her the cuff links. "It's difficult to see in this light, but does that look like the initials A.C.?"

She inspected the links. "The letters are worn, but yeah. The C's clearer than the A."

"Alan Cargill," Zack said. The late owner of Cargill Racing.

Gaby gasped. "These are his?"

"He wore them at every major occasion. Including last year's banquet." Where Alan had been killed, and where his watch and cuff links had gone missing.

They stared at each other, processing the implication. It seemed one person among this glittering crowd knew more about Alan's death than they'd admitted.

"We have to tell the police," Gaby said, shaken.

Zack nodded. "I think that detective, Lucas Haines, is still on the case. Chad will have his number—Haines interviewed him at one point." Carefully he wrapped the tissue around the cuff links. "Unfortunately, we probably just obscured any fingerprints that might have been on them." He put the package into his pocket. "I guess Haines will want to interview both of us. We might need to set aside some time tomorrow."

"He'll probably want to know exactly what we were doing in here." Gaby ran her hands over her hair, smoothing it down. Her primping reminded Zack how it felt to have his hands buried in there, cupping her head.

"I'm sure he's heard more shocking confessions," he said. "I doubt we'll make the front pages." He paused. "Headline-worthy though that kiss was."

She pinkened. "It was," she agreed.

He kissed her again. "Hold that thought. I plan to do it again very soon."

CHAPTER TWELVE

AMBER HELD HER WINEGLASS out in front of her in an attempt to create some personal space in the crowded museum. She shouldn't have agreed to her mom's request that she attend Patsy Grosso's party.

It felt as if she was swimming in a sea of betrayal. Many of the people in this room had known her father, but as far as she knew, none of them had lifted a finger to help Julie-Anne. She wondered which of them had abetted her father's addiction to alcohol. Somebody had supplied Billy with liquor after his accident, and it wasn't Julie-Anne.

She glanced around for someone she might be able to trust. Chad and Brianna were dancing; Zack and Gaby appeared to be leaving in a hurry. Amber's mom was at the other end of the room. She and Brady were caught up in a discussion with team owner Adam Sanford. Amber watched them. Did Brady's grip on Julie-Anne's arm look more than possessive…?

"Evening, beautiful," said a familiar voice.

Amber never would have thought she'd be pleased to see Ryan. "You again," she said with feigned irritation. She found herself smiling as she turned…and caught her breath.

Unlike most of the men present, he wore a tuxedo. Not stiffly, but with a careless grace that said he could get away with wearing it to a cookout if he chose. His blondish hair was rumpled—not like the other morning when he'd just woken up—as if he'd worked on messing it up just right. The effect was gorgeous.

Ryan measured her interest in his appearance, and grinned. "Don't tell me I've caught your attention at last?"

"I was bored," she said.

Ryan laughed. Did he take anything seriously? Amber had to wonder.

"I'm not so proud that I won't settle for that. Let's take a walk," he said.

She needed to stop spying on her mom, and she desperately wanted to get away from the crowd of people who'd known her father. Ryan was surely too young to remember her dad as anything more than a name in the race program.

She tucked her hand through the arm he offered.

Danger. Her senses flashed a warning, bells went off in her head. Maybe she was especially vulnerable tonight, with these thoughts of the past and of her father, but touching Ryan felt more dangerous than canyoning or blackwater rafting, or any of the extreme things she'd done in her job as an adventure travel guide.

Ryan's blue eyes darkened, and his other hand closed over hers where it rested on his arm. "Let's go, before you change your mind."

Barely able to think, Amber went with him, letting him use his bulk to move her through the crowd that a minute ago had been too close, but that now seemed to part obligingly.

"You look stunning." He glanced back at her, at her red dress, which made the most of her curves.

She didn't want his flattery, she only wanted him to hold her close, to protect her. *Stupid. He's a serial flirt, he thinks any woman is lucky to have his attention.* Though she had discovered that Libby, the team receptionist, was indeed passionate about recycling—Amber had been wrong to suggest Ryan was using her as some kind of servant.

Several women brushed deliberately against him as they progressed through the room. Vexed that she was no more immune than they were, she said, "How many women have you said that to tonight?"

Annoyance flitted across his face. "You're the first."

"If it doesn't work with me, will you try it on someone else?"

RYAN WAS TEMPTED TO let go of Amber and walk away. What was with the massive chip on her shoulder?

He ignored the fact that with another woman, he might well have given up at such a contrary response, and found someone more willing to play the flirtation game. She had no right to make that assumption about him. But since walking away would just prove her point, he decided to stay.

"I've been thinking about you," he said.

She cocked her head and raised her eyebrows, her skepticism blatant.

He steered her into the museum's internal courtyard, open to the night sky. He figured the concrete bench seat would be cold enough that she'd need to snuggle closer to him. He shrugged out of his jacket and laid it down for her to sit on.

"Thanks," Amber said. "But your chivalry won't change anything—I don't want to date you."

Ryan gave her an injured look. "My mind isn't a single-groove race track, you know. I brought you out here so you can tell me more about your travels."

She laughed; he detected relief in it. "No one wants to hear about other people's travels," she said.

"Seriously," he insisted. "I've never been farther than Montreal, for the NASCAR Nationwide Series race. I always planned to travel, but I haven't gotten to it yet." He spread his hands disarmingly. "Educate me."

"Travel is something you have to do for yourself," she said. He could tell she was trying very hard not to be won over.

"What's your favorite place on earth?"

"Cappadocia, in Turkey," she said instantly, as if she considered the question on a daily basis.

"The place with those weird rock pillars?"

She looked insultingly surprised that he knew it. "They have so much history," she said, "yet they'd be equally incredible if they just sprang up tomorrow."

She looked incredible, her blue eyes alight with awe, no longer shadowed by whatever had been bothering her. Her mouth was full and perfect. She got under Ryan's skin like no one he could remember.

He touched her cheek with one finger. Amber stilled. Then she relaxed. "You're very young," she said, as if that somehow made him not a threat.

"Very," Ryan agreed, willing to play along if it meant he got to touch her cheek again. Or more. "How old are you, exactly?"

"I told you. Way, way too old."

"Hmm." His hand found the back of her neck, his thumb moved over the tender nape. She drew in a breath. "Pity," he murmured.

Reluctantly, he made the strategic decision not to kiss her. She'd made it clear she didn't trust him. Rushing her would reinforce that judgment.

"We should go get another drink." He tugged Amber to her feet, and noted the disappointment in her eyes. Mingled with relief. Man, this was one complicated woman. Couldn't she just want to kiss him, the way he did her?

As they headed down the short corridor back to the main room, a man rushed past them, smacking into Amber and sending her crashing into Ryan. The guy—Tony Winters, Ryan saw now—snarled something that definitely wasn't an apology, and hurried on.

"You okay?" Ryan grasped Amber's shoulders…and was shocked at the contempt in her eyes.

"What a creep," she said. "I'll bet he shoves other people out of his way when he's on the track."

Something snapped inside Ryan. "What is it with you?" he demanded. "That was Tony Winters—he's an accountant, for Pete's sake, I doubt he's ever been near a race car." He released her, took a step back. "You think 'slick guys—'" he made finger quotes "—like me are secret monsters, you think the gruff, unpolished guys like Brady are secret bullies. Get over it, Amber."

Her eyes sparked, and her chest rose and fell distractingly. "Don't tell me what to do."

Oh, yeah, Ms. Independence to the end.

"Can't you accept that sometimes, things *are* what they seem?" Ryan thought about her response to his compliment on her appearance earlier. "Not everything has to be a big damn deal," he ranted. "Sometimes, flirting is just flirting. Kissing is just kissing."

He realized she wasn't listening. That her eyes had got hung up on his lips. He took that as a cue to prove his point.

He put his hands to Amber's waist, lowered his mouth to hers.

Soft, sexy, voluptuous. Kissing Amber was like tumbling into a new realm that made everything in his life to date feel like a mere practice for the real thing. Ryan couldn't get enough. He teased her with his tongue, felt her response— hesitant at first, then more assertive. She kissed like the kind of woman she was—confident, yet conflicted. It made for delicious torment.

Ryan deepened the kiss. He pulled her against him, reveled in her soft curves. His hands found her derriere. Mmm.

What happened to kissing is just kissing? a tiny voice asked inside his head. Because this wasn't *just* anything.

The thought was enough to make him pull back, to remind him of the decision he'd made back when his race results first went south. Rule number one: no distractions.

With great reluctance, he eased away from Amber. Her cheeks were flushed, her hair tousled. She looked the way he'd imagined she would in bed.

He meant to make a snappy comment about having proved his point, but all that came out was a hoarse "Ah…"

Amber stared at him, wide-eyed. Then she whirled away, and almost sprinted back to the party. This was getting to be a familiar sight, Amber running from him. He should be relieved…but he wasn't.

ZACK HAD INVITED GABY to have dinner with him the night before the race at Michigan, right after a *Now Woman*'s bachelor contest reader party being held at the track. This time she accepted the dinner invitation—it was either that, or she risked exploding from frustration. Zack had told her to "hold that thought" of the kiss they'd shared at Patsy's party, and in the days that followed, she'd thought of little else.

But that was as far as things had gone. Zack had been honoring his commitment to the Canine Rescue Foundation, shooting an ad to support its Christmas fund-raising. Gaby had been called in to help a colleague deal with a crisis over another driver.

She'd talked to Zack on the phone, but, chatty guy that he wasn't, it had been less than satisfactory. So she jumped at the chance of dinner.

She wanted off the roller coaster and into the tunnel of love.

From the way Zack had stood up for her in the meeting with Getaway, she figured she didn't need to worry that he might pressure her into giving up her ambitions. Which meant there was no reason why she couldn't date him…but it would be best to keep it from Sandra. Because there was definite conflict between Motor Media Group's priority—keeping Getaway Resorts happy—and Zack's priority, which was to focus on his racing. Sandra might worry that Gaby would act against the company's interest. Gaby knew she wouldn't.

She stood alongside him as he greeted *Now Woman*'s readers. Anyone would think there was a severe shortage of men on the planet, going by the way some of these women threw themselves at him.

There was, Gaby supposed, a severe shortage of men like Zack.

"Don't these ladies know you have a race tomorrow?" she asked, as Zack declined what must have been the tenth not-so-subtle invitation to enjoy some late-night activities with a blonde bombshell.

He looked at her in surprise. Then a slow smile widened his mouth. "Maybe I need to make that clearer."

She gritted her teeth as a bevy of beauties called out to Zack, then rushed over to him. Every single one was blonde, tanned, gorgeous. Was there some kind of cloning program going on? Was it too late for Gaby to sign up?

I don't need a tan or blond hair to run Motor Media Group, she reminded herself.

She kept a strictly professional eye on Zack while he socialized. He didn't appear to be flirting with anyone, but how many gorgeous women could one race car driver reasonably be expected to resist?

Maybe she should call the restaurant and asked to be seated next to someone superfrumpy.

At eight o'clock, Zack had fulfilled his obligations and was free to go. He stayed close to Gaby as they walked to her rental car.

"My, what a lot of fans you have," she said.

He slid her a sidelong glance. "All the better to wow my sponsor with."

"Hey, you two," a voice called as Gaby pressed the button to unlock her car. She turned to see Trent and Kelly approaching.

"What are you doing here?" Zack asked his brother. "You're not a bachelor."

"Damn right," Trent said with satisfaction. He kissed Kelly to prove it. "We had a couple of drinks and a pizza in town, took a taxi back. Now we're headed back to the motor home."

Zack squared his shoulders. "Well done on qualifying yesterday," he said. Trent had qualified ninth for Sunday's race, against Zack's eighteenth.

"Thanks," Trent said, surprised.

But Zack wasn't done. "I heard your car was running loose, which means your qualifying time was quite an achievement. I'll have my work cut out catching up to you."

Silence fell, in Gaby's case due to a pride and tenderness that clogged her throat.

Trent said to Gaby, "Who is this smooth talker and what did you do with my sandpaper brother?"

Zack laughed along with everyone. Kelly grabbed her husband's arm. "Trent's going to quit while he's ahead," she announced.

"But, sugar, I was just warming up." Trent's plaintive protest drew more laughter, a warmth that lingered after the couples had parted and stayed with Gaby and Zack all the way to the restaurant.

They followed the maître d' past a group of drivers and crew chiefs from Fulcrum Racing, who were engrossed in a heated discussion of track conditions. Zack half looked as if he'd like to stop and join in, but he headed with Gaby for the table they'd been given in the middle of the room. The maître d' handed them their menus and took the wine order. After he left, an awkward silence fell.

Gaby found herself feeling shy. Which was crazy, after all the time she'd spent with Zack recently. She glanced around. The table next to them was empty. No frumpy woman, but no nubile blonde, either.

"Your dress is pretty," he said.

"Thanks." Self-conscious, Gaby smoothed the empire line skirt that flared out softly from her black dress's halter top. It was a flattering style, baring her shoulders and gathering under her bust in a way that emphasized the curves.

Zack leaned forward. "Normally I love my job, but this week I've hated everything that's kept me apart from you."

Coming from Zack, whose job was his life, it felt like the nicest thing anyone had ever said to her. Her awkwardness slipped away. "Me, too," she said. "I came so close to telling Anita to get a grip and look after her own darn client."

He took her hand, and the simple contact locked them into a world of their own. He smiled, and his eyes lightened. Gaby knew their every fleck and shadow. Just like she knew the contour of the mouth below them, and the strength in the fingers that wrapped around hers.

The restaurant seemed suddenly warmer. With her free hand, Gaby took a drink of her water.

"This thing between us," Zack said. "I have a feeling it could be serious, Gaby."

She sputtered on her water. "Excuse me?"

"It's not...it's not just a regular attraction." He sat back while the waiter poured their wine.

They chose their meals from the menu. When the waiter left, she said, "You're right."

Since her broken engagement, she'd been cautious. But what she felt for Zack couldn't be denied. She doused a flicker of concern over what Sandra would think, and touched Zack's hand. That excited, boyish look she was crazy about came over his face.

Just then someone brushed past Gaby's chair. Three men whom Gaby recognized sat down at the table next to theirs.

"Hi, Zack," Danny Cruise said.

With an apologetic glance at Gaby, Zack stood to greet Danny, a friend of his, along with his crew chief and team owner. Danny nodded at Gaby—he was a client of Motor Media Group, so he knew her by sight.

"Madison not with you tonight?" Zack asked. Everyone knew Danny seldom went anywhere without the wife he adored.

Just the mention of her name brought a goofy smile to the man's face. "She's back in the motor home, she's tired out." Danny paused. "I'm allowed to tell you all now—we're expecting a baby."

The casual words didn't fool Gaby—Danny was bursting with pride. Zack congratulated his friend and did a pretty good job of asking the right questions.

It was a few minutes before he sat back down with Gaby. In the moment of silence before they resumed their conversation, Gaby heard Danny and his colleagues get immersed into a discussion of tomorrow's race.

"Danny's always had an uncanny level of focus," she said.

"Which might explain why he wins more races than I do." Zack darted a tormented glance at Danny's table.

"Do you want to go home and work on the race?" she asked.

"I want to be with you," he said. "Alone with you."

Alone was a great idea. Gaby was starting to worry that with Danny at the next table, word of her dinner with Zack would get back to Sandra. Not that dinner with a client was a problem. It was the holding hands and the intense looks that would provoke speculation. They had to get out of here, away from Danny Cruise, from the Fulcrum Racing guys who were making more noise than anyone else in the restaurant, from the several other tables she now saw were occupied by NASCAR folk, albeit they were people she didn't really know. Away from the intrusion of the reality of Zack's job as a NASCAR driver.

"We could go back to my hotel," she said.

Zack needed no encouragement. He signaled for the check and refused the waiter's offer to package up their almost-ready meals. Five minutes later they were out on the sidewalk, where they literally almost ran in to Sandra and Gideon Taney, arriving for dinner.

Zack cursed. Gaby tugged the lapels of her jacket together as she greeted her boss. "This place is popular with NASCAR people tonight," she said. *Calm, professional, nothing going on here.*

"They sneaked a bunch of flyers into the motor home lot," Taney said. "We're all too lazy to look any further."

"Would you two like to join us for a drink?" Sandra asked.

"We have plans," Zack said.

"We're reviewing tonight's bachelor contest event," Gaby said hastily.

Sandra gave Gaby an approving look. She'd adopted flat shoes for the later part of her pregnancy, and with Gaby wearing high-heeled sandals, they were closer in height than usual.

"I have some news," Sandra said. "It looks as if I'll be stopping work sooner than planned."

"Is something wrong?" Gaby asked, concerned.

Sandra rubbed the small of her back. "My blood pressure's up. Not too much at this point, but the doctor says it'll likely go higher. She wants me to stop work in late September."

The baby was due mid-December, conveniently timed, Gaby assumed, for the end of the NASCAR season.

"Which means," Sandra said, "I'll be appointing my successor around the Richmond race, to allow a couple of weeks for handover."

Gaby did the mental calculation. That gave her three weeks to convince Sandra she should have the promotion.

She traded a glance with Zack. He was already on tenterhooks about the Richmond race, the last one before the Chase for the NASCAR Sprint Cup. Now she was, too.

"We need to go," Zack said apologetically to the Taneys. He practically hustled her to her car in his haste to get away. She wondered if he felt the same way she did—reluctant to think about the fact that they were each headed for Richmond with different priorities.

CHAPTER THIRTEEN

ZACK HURRIED GABY UP to her hotel room with the desperate eagerness of a rookie to make his first pass. How long was it since he'd felt this excited about kissing a woman? Making love with a woman? Hell, just *being* with this woman was enough. Now that he thought about it, Zack wasn't sure he'd ever felt like this.

In the elevator, he caught Gaby in his arms. "You drive me crazy," he said.

"Good," she said, with such relief that he laughed.

"And you make me laugh." He definitely couldn't think of another woman who'd done that.

"You have a wonderful laugh," she said.

"I do?"

"Wonderful," she said firmly. "I love it."

"I love doing this," Zack said, and he kissed her.

Her response was so heated, he wanted the elevator journey to never end. When it did, he whisked her along the hallway and they fell into her room, lips locked together. Mmm, Gaby tasted so sweet, like honey.

Zack tugged her closer, felt those dangerous curves of hers snug against him. His hands moved over her, exploring, at first gentle, then bolder, pressing, molding.

Gaby's hands on his back grew more insistent, Zack's possession of her mouth more intimate.

"I want you," he murmured into the curve of her neck, "so much it scares me."

She turned her head, giving him access to her ear. She gasped as his tongue found that sweet spot. "I can't believe we're actually doing this," she said breathlessly.

"Mmm." He nuzzled her red-gold curls.

"I'm so glad you got over that anti-career-woman thing."

"Uh, yeah." He wasn't entirely sure what she was talking about, but he knew he didn't want it getting in the way.

Gaby must have picked up on his distraction. "You did, didn't you?"

He kissed her mouth again, silencing her. It worked for all of ten seconds.

She put her hands to his chest, gave a little push that was a clear signal to stop. Zack eased away from her mouth.

"You don't still have a view that you can only marry someone who doesn't have a career, do you?" she asked.

Every instinct Zack possessed protested against talking about marriage on a first date. "I never said that," he disagreed. "I mean, sure, I'd expect my wife to make a home for us, but that doesn't mean she can't work."

"It takes two to make a home."

His arms slackened around her waist. "But while I'm racing NASCAR I'm pretty tied up. My wife would likely end up in charge of creating the home. It's hard to see two really demanding careers fitting into one marriage."

Gaby drew a sharp breath. "*I* have a really demanding career."

He released her. "Gaby, we're on our first date. I'm not sure this is relevant."

"You said it feels serious. I don't want to get close to you, then find out it can't go anywhere." She sat on the end of the bed.

"It's not as if I'm saying my wife's career would be over the day she married me," Zack said, frustrated. "A guy can't race NASCAR forever."

"Dean Grosso raced until he was fifty. I imagine you haven't set a time limit on your racing."

Hell, no. Zack admired the way Grosso had hung in there, winning the NASCAR Sprint Cup Series championship right before he retired.

"Dean did race a long time," he admitted. "Patsy made a fulfilling career out of supporting her husband." He was arguably doing a disservice to Patsy Grosso, an active co-owner of Cargill-Grosso Racing, but, heck, he had a point to make.

"Dean and Patsy split up last year," Gaby said.

"They got back together again." He thought about sitting next to her on the bed, maybe trying to get those kisses going again.

"So, your ideal wife will put her career on hold for you. Or make you her career."

"I want to marry someone who loves me enough to put our marriage first," he said.

"While you put it second."

"It's not like that," he said, exasperated. "I grew up sidelined in my family. I don't want to start a marriage in the same place. Is that so bad?"

She folded her arms across her chest, putting up a shield that made it clear he wasn't welcome to join her on the bed. "I was forced to choose between love and my career once," she said. "Never again."

Zack leaned against the TV cabinet. "You're talking about your engagement." Now this, he did want to hear.

She nodded. "Sandra offered me a promotion to account director. My fiancé asked me to refuse it. He was worried I wouldn't have time for our relationship. For him."

Zack was torn. He recognized the unreasonable nature of the demand, yet he understood it, too.

"I decided our future was more important than my work, so I turned down the promotion," Gaby said. "Three months later, he left me for another woman."

Zack cursed. "Jerk. You're better off without him."

"It didn't feel that way at the time."

"I wouldn't leave a woman who made that kind of sacrifice for me," he said.

"But shouldn't marriage be both people making sacrifices?"

Zack frowned. Ideally, marriage shouldn't be a sacrifice at all. It should be something two people went into because they loved each other. "I guess," he said, feeling his way, "maybe both sides need to give and take." *Sides*. Sounded like a war.

"If I fell in love with a man like you," she said, her color high, "it would be all-consuming."

Sounded good to Zack.

"Unless you felt the same way, which it's clear you don't," she said, "I'd end up doing all the giving and you'd be doing all the taking."

"That's not how it would be." He fumbled for an explanation that sounded reasonable…but something about having her so close, with her red-gold curls tumbling around her shoulders, her fair skin an alluring contrast to her black dress, was scrambling his brain.

"All I'm saying—" he brought it back to the core truth, one even Gaby couldn't argue with "—is that to race NASCAR, you have to be single-minded. Even if you're not actually single."

Gaby's eyes widened as she absorbed that. "And all I'm saying," she said, "is that I want a man I can love, but not one I'll love too much."

"How can you love someone too much?" he demanded.

"I don't want to love someone more than he loves me," she amended.

"Gaby, this is crazy," he said. "We have something special, we owe it to ourselves to explore it. If it doesn't work out—if I lose focus on my driving or you think you're losing your independence—then it'll come to a natural end."

She plucked at the duvet with her fingers. "I don't think I can take the risk, not now. Sandra isn't convinced I can have a relationship without it interfering in the running of Motor

Media. If you and I were dating…I don't think she'd trust I could handle the conflict of interest."

"Of course you could," Zack said.

"Could I?" Her gaze met his. "How would you feel about my divided loyalties?"

"I wouldn't…I…" Zack ran a hand through his hair. Her career was already coming between them? This was unbelievable. "What are you saying? That we're finished before we began?"

"I'm saying I don't want to throw away everything I've worked for, for a man who doesn't want to give as much to the relationship as I do." She blinked hard, as if fighting tears.

It sounded like they were finished to him. But he still wanted to kiss her. Make love with her. He was damned if he was going to miss out on that. "I understand you're under pressure with Sandra," he said with an effort. "But what we've got, I don't want to let it go so easily."

"Me, neither," she admitted quietly.

Okay, that was better. The pain Zack hadn't realized he had in his chest eased. He took her hands in his. "It's only three weeks until Richmond, until Sandra makes her decision. How about we put us on hold until then?"

"You'd do that?" Her eyes brightened.

"See, I'm making allowances for your career already." Zack felt pretty pleased with himself.

"It would be a relief not to worry about Sandra getting suspicious," she said.

He pulled her to her feet and kissed her lightly on the lips. "It'll be frustrating as heck, but we can wait three weeks, right?"

"Sure. I think. Thank you, Zack." She kissed him back, and as always the heat was instantaneous and insatiable. The kiss deepened, but just when Zack thought things might get interesting, she drew away. "Three weeks," she promised. "Then we'll figure out if we can make this work."

AMBER HAD EXPECTED STAYING in Brady's motor home at Bristol with him and her mom to be cramped and awkward. But Julie-Anne had insisted with rare firmness.

Luckily, the motor home was as big as they came, and her mother and Brady had a separate bedroom with a king-size bed, while Amber took the smaller bedroom at the back.

"Honey, would you like a cup of pumpkin soup?" Julie-Anne asked. She had always been a great cook, fond of experimenting.

"You used to make chicken noodle soup with homemade noodles," Amber remembered.

Julie-Anne tensed. "I stopped when your father had his accident."

"I didn't mean…" Amber had been trying to dig up a happy memory to share with Julie-Anne, but it sounded like an accusation of neglect. Had she subconsciously meant it that way?

"Billy was never one to appreciate the effort that went into preparing a meal," Julie-Anne said.

Amber analyzed her mom's tone and detected only neutrality. No love for her first husband, but no hatred, either.

Amber hated Billy Blake.

"Here." Julie-Anne held out a mug of soup.

Amber sipped, careful not to burn herself. Mmm, she tasted cardamom. "Great," she said.

The door opened and Brady stuck his head in. "I can smell that soup clear from Chad's place."

"Come in and I'll fix you a cup," Julie-Anne said.

Brady stepped inside and wrapped his arms around his wife. "A culinary genius and gorgeous to boot," he said. "How did I get so lucky?"

"Lucky dog rule," Julie-Anne said, a teasing reference to the NASCAR rule that gave a second chance to a driver who'd fallen off the lead lap.

"I sure am." Brady kissed her. Then he saw Amber watching and ended the kiss, though he didn't release Julie-Anne.

Amber smiled at him—the first genuine warm smile she'd given him since she'd arrived. She didn't remember her father ever having one nice word to say to her mom...or to her. Brady might be a little controlling, but his sons could still tell him to back off, and he appreciated Julie-Anne. Amber wasn't looking for a stepfather, but maybe this was a guy she could trust with her mom. Maybe.

Brady grinned back at her, less guarded than he usually seems. "I got you something."

"You didn't need to," she said.

"You'll love it, it's a giant panda."

"Um, that's, gosh, Brady, that's…"

Brady roared with laughter. "It's not a panda, honey."

Honey? She grinned sheepishly. "You can't blame me for being worried."

"This is something I hope you'll like better." He pulled an envelope from his pocket, handed it over.

Amber lifted the flap, peeked inside. "A NASCAR pass?"

"A hard-card," Brady said. "It says you're a member of our team."

Amber inspected the hard-card, which bore the Matheson Racing name.

"I know how you feel about racing," Brady said. "But it's a big part of your mom's life. I'm a big part of her life, too, and I'm a NASCAR man through and through. You don't ever have to come to another race if you don't want to. But this—" he indicated the hard-card "—is here for you if you want it, and so is the team. Matheson Racing is yours as much as mine and your mom's, as much as the boys'. You're family, Amber."

She blinked rapidly. "Brady, that's very sweet. Thank you."

"Oh, honey." Julie-Anne hugged Brady, then Amber, and for a moment it looked as if all three of them would be in tears.

A knock at the motor home door dissolved the tension.

"Come in," Brady called.

Ryan entered. "Hello, sir," he said. He nodded to Julie-Anne. "Mrs. Matheson."

Amber's stomach flipped. "What are you doing here?" After she'd run away from Patsy's party, he'd backed right off. He'd been polite at work, but he'd given no clues he wanted to kiss her again. Which, she had to admit, she regretted. She hadn't been able to forget that kiss, and she was starting to think she was being unreasonable to assume the worst just because he was handsome and personable.

Her unintentional abruptness had Brady and Julie-Anne staring. But Ryan turned on that cocky grin of his.

"Hey, Amber. My motor home is only a block away," he said, deliberately misunderstanding her question.

"Well…hi," Amber said, aware her mother was waiting to see some common courtesy.

"I was just wondering if you might want to come back to my place for a drink?" He was still grinning, but there was something in his eyes she hadn't seen before. Was it…insecurity?

"Don't you have a race to run tonight?" she asked.

"I meant a soda. Or coffee."

She'd missed him, missed talking to him, missed his attentions. "I guess I could," she said casually.

Brady stepped forward. "Are your folks there, Ryan?"

Amber blinked. Brady sounded for all the world as if he might pull out a shotgun if Ryan's intentions weren't pure. As if he was *protecting* her. Something softened in her chest.

Julie-Anne rolled her eyes. "Amber's twenty-nine, Brady."

Ryan gasped with feigned shock, and Amber stuck out her tongue at him, more like a ten-year-old than a woman who was too old for a bratty race car driver.

"My mom's in," he told Brady. "It's my parents' motor home, so I have to share it with them." Many of the NASCAR Nationwide Series drivers didn't have their own motor homes, Amber knew.

She couldn't figure Ryan out. He was flirtatious as heck, clearly knew his way around a woman. Not to mention he was funny, polite when he chose to be and kissed like a dream. Yet for a guy who could have any woman he wanted, he sure was persistent where Amber was concerned. As if he really did like her. And now he planned to introduce her to his mom. Amber's father had been estranged from his family. Was this more evidence she could trust Ryan?

"I'll be fine, thank you, Brady," she said.

Ryan held out a hand, and she took it. He laced his fingers through Amber's with a firmness that suggested he wasn't about to let her go.

As they left, Brady said, "Ryan?"

"Yes, sir?" Ryan faced him.

"Just remember that's my family you're holding hands with."

"Yes, sir," Ryan said, with more seriousness than Amber knew he had in him.

HOLDING AMBER'S HAND had the very pleasant effect of dulling Ryan's memories of last week's NASCAR Nationwide Series race in Michigan. He'd finished the race, but that was the best thing that could be said about it. His dad had been over the moon when Ryan had qualified third, but car setup problems resulted in a washout twenty-third finish. It would've almost been better to have crashed, preferably while attempting a daring pass that would have had the commentators yelling themselves hoarse, and ended the race with at least some glory.

Ryan sighed.

"What's the matter?" Amber asked. "Didn't you really want me to come for a drink or not?"

He firmed his grip on her. She was the touchiest gal he'd ever met—if he loosened off, she'd probably run away again. "I wouldn't have asked if I didn't want you." He deliberately didn't add *to come for a drink.* Because there was a whole lot he wanted Amber for, and a drink was the least of it.

He was taking a risk making his intentions so plain, given her refusal to date drivers. But she seemed softer today, somehow. Her lips quirked in a reluctant smile, and she didn't give him a verbal slapdown. Excitement coursed through Ryan. Too bad his mom was waiting back at the motor home.

"I'm sorry about your finish in last week's race," Amber said. "I should have said something sooner."

"You're not being nice because you feel sorry for me, are you?" he said, appalled.

"Of course not." She walked a few more steps. "I wasn't intending to be nice at all."

Ah, that was more like the Amber he knew. Ryan found himself grinning inside. "So," he said, "twenty-nine, huh?"

She pffed.

"I could have sworn you were trying to make me feel as if you're ten years older than I am."

"I'm ten years more mature," she said. "That's what matters."

He chuckled.

"See," she said, "you laugh at everything, like a kid."

"Not everything," he said sourly, and wished he hadn't. Thankfully, the motor home was in sight.

But Amber stopped. "Tell me."

He stopped too, and when he met her eyes, he forgot about the motor homes around them, the smell of barbecue, the squeals of kids playing. His gut tightened. Damn but he liked Amber, sharp edges and all.

"Tonight's race," he said. "Dad and Grandad will be sitting up on the hauler, Granded clutching his chest every time someone passes me." Ryan hoped he'd delivered that with the lightheartedness she'd been teasing him about.

To his surprise, she took his other hand in hers. Her fingers were slender but strong.

"It's only one race," she said.

"One race that I can't afford to have end like some of the others have. I qualified twenty-third." His shoulders sagged.

"I need to finish in the top five in the Nationwide Series if I want to get a Sprint Cup ride next year."

She squirmed, and he had the sense she was slipping away. He held a little tighter.

"And is that what you want?" she asked.

It was weird, having their most personal conversation to date in the middle of a crowded motor home lot. But if they'd been alone, talking would have been the last thing on his mind. And for some reason, Amber had lowered her defenses. He was determined to keep them down.

"I want to race in the Sprint Cup," he admitted. "My folks are desperate for me to win the Nationwide Series, too." He saw her frown. "My dad won it twenty-two years ago," he explained, "and my granddad won twenty years before that. It's a big deal to them."

"And to you?"

"And to me. Of course."

"I hope you make it, then." From her, the sentiment didn't seem like a platitude, and it certainly wasn't the kind of glib assurance he hated. No, it seemed as if Amber understood something about what it was to be pinned down by history.

Ryan leaned forward and kissed her lips. Almost chastely, given their public location, but not quite, because Amber was way too hot to confine himself to chaste. She kissed him back—she tasted sweet and true.

The hooting of a couple of kids parted them. She was smiling…a secretive, cat's smile that made Ryan want to take her somewhere very private. He sighed. "Let's go see Mom."

AMBER TURNED UP IN Ryan's pits just before the race. Given she wasn't a big race fan, he had to be the reason she was there. He excused himself from his crew chief, and smirked as he walked up to her.

She gave him her customary scowl, but he could tell her heart wasn't in it. He kissed her.

"Mmmf." She gave a protest that he stifled with his mouth on hers. Then she kissed him back. Sweet. Oh, yeah.

Ryan was almost shaking when he pulled away. That couldn't be good before a race, one part of his mind said. The other part urged him to kiss her again.

Amber wrapped her arms around herself as if she, too, was none too steady. But when she spoke, her voice had its usual mix of sweetness and challenge. "Are you ready?"

"I guess," he said. He wasn't looking forward to watching the tails of the twenty-two other cars in front of him when they started.

"It doesn't matter," she said.

He laughed. "Better not let my dad hear that. You'd probably get kicked out for heresy."

"When you were talking earlier about your dad and your granddad and their expectations," she said, "it made me think about the baggage my mom and I have."

"Yeah?"

"You have to figure out why you're holding on to it, and if it's worth holding on to."

"Right," he said, with no idea what she meant.

"The race doesn't matter," she said again. "Not as much as plenty of other things." She went up on tiptoe, kissed his chin, then left the pits without looking back.

Ryan shook his head. She was killing him, and he was loving every minute.

A short time later as he started his engine in response to the grand marshal's command, he wondered how the heck he was supposed to concentrate on the half-mile track's tight turns and straightaways when the only curve on his mind was the curve of Amber's lips.

His driving was mechanical, barely focused on the race—which was insane, given how close the racing action was at Bristol. After fifty laps he couldn't have said where he sat in the pack. At the halfway mark, still cursing his inability to let go of Amber. Suddenly he realized his dad sounded excited.

"Where are we sitting, Dad?" he asked.

"I just told you," his father said. "Fifth."

Fifth! Ryan got such a shock he almost let Roberto Castillo—*hell, I'm in front of Castillo*—pass him. Just in time, he cut the former open-wheel racing champion off, and heard his father's yell of triumph through his earpiece.

But not even his elation over his current performance could keep Amber out of Ryan's mind for long, and he soon found his concentration drifting again.

But he did happen to register that he crossed the line in second place, his best result this season.

His father and his grandfather were beside themselves with excitement. "The way you finessed Castillo reminded me of how I held off Dean Grosso in the final race when I won the series," his father crowed.

Ryan figured his father's statement was a compliment. He said something back, but he wasn't sure what. He needed to see Amber. He'd hoped she'd be waiting for him in the pits, ready to share the thrill.

But he wasn't surprised when she wasn't.

Unpredictable woman, his Amber. The flash of possession surprised him—he wasn't prone to clinging to his girlfriends. Hey, he'd just come second in a NASCAR Nationwide Series race. Small wonder he felt as if he owned the world.

CHAPTER FOURTEEN

"I CAN'T FIGURE OUT how I did so well when I wasn't even concentrating," Ryan said to Kelly Matheson the next day. He'd paid her a visit in her and Trent's motor home to talk about the race. "Everyone knows winning a NASCAR race takes incredible focus."

She crossed her legs and swung her foot as she thought. "People focus in different ways, at different levels. Sometimes, your subconscious is more focused than you are at a conscious level."

"That sounds complicated," Ryan said. "Hard to replicate." Because that was what he needed to do. Figure out what went right at Bristol, then do the same next weekend in Montreal. And the weekend after, and the weekend after that.

"What did you do differently ahead of yesterday's race?" Kelly asked. She was big on honing prerace routines so that you only did what worked, however whacky it might sound, and got rid of the ineffective stuff. Trent had experienced a huge turnaround in his racing after he'd bought in to Kelly's strategy.

"The only thing I did different—" he'd already thought about this "—was that I kissed a girl."

A smile played on Kelly's lips. "I'm certain I've seen you kissing a girl ahead of a race before. Many girls."

He might have known she wouldn't let him get away with that statement. "Maybe the difference is the girl," he said. "Amber."

Her eyebrows rose, and he wondered if that was sympathy he saw in her expression. Sympathy because Brady would have his hide if he messed around with his stepdaughter, or because Amber wasn't the easiest woman in the world? Ryan didn't care about either of those.

"Was it the first time you've kissed her?" Kelly asked.

Ryan shoved his hands in his pockets. He hoped she was bound by professional ethics not to mention this to her husband or any of her in-laws. "The first time before a race," he clarified.

"Uh-huh." She made a few notes, but didn't say anything else.

"I couldn't stop thinking about it when I was driving," Ryan said.

She grinned. "Some kiss, huh?"

He sighed. "Yeah. But, you know, not in that obvious way."

"Interesting," Kelly murmured.

"I've certainly never analyzed a kiss this much before," he admitted.

"So, what made this one so special?"

"You're asking that as my shrink, right? Not just because you're nosy."

"Of course," she said, suspiciously wide-eyed. Still, she was the best person to talk to about this.

"Here's how I see it," Ryan said. "Last year, I dated a lot of women."

"All those prerace kisses I saw."

"Yeah. As you know, I had a so-so season. My father said I was fooling around too much, I had to cool it with the girls."

"So this season…" Kelly prompted.

"This season, I haven't dated anyone at all." He hadn't actually missed the stream of women, either. "But all that extra focus hasn't helped my racing. If anything, it's been worse."

"Maybe you needed to lighten up," Kelly said.

Exactly the conclusion he'd come to. "I think it's about

balance," he agreed. "Not so many women that there's no consistency in my life, but nothing so serious that it takes me away from my racing."

Kelly frowned. "I get the not-so-many-women aspect, but where did the nothing serious idea come from? You haven't actually tried a serious relationship, have you?"

"Not my kind of thing," he said. He'd never had a relationship he could call serious, couldn't see himself wanting one in the near future. "But if I could have a—a semirelationship with Amber, it might be what my racing needs."

"A semirelationship," Kelly said bemused.

"Uh-huh." He'd been thinking about this nonstop. Now that he'd said it, he knew he was right.

"You could give it a try, I suppose," Kelly said. "If you're sure you don't want to go the whole way and get serious."

"Amber's not exactly an easy person, and I get enough relationship pressure and expectations from my family." He'd told her some of those problems before.

"Did you think about tackling those family pressures, rather than pinning your hopes on a semigirlfriend?" Kelly never shied away from the difficult questions.

"I can't change my folks," Ryan said. "I can't turn them around this far into the season. The girlfriend side is easier to manage, as long as I keep it light, like you said."

"Is that what I said?" Kelly's smile was a mix of amusement and sympathy. Then she sobered. "It's your decision, Ryan, whether you tackle the underlying problem of your family's expectations, or whether you seek to minimize that pressure by finding relaxation elsewhere. But if you decide you want to get closer to Amber, can I suggest you find a different way of thinking about it? And certainly of phrasing it. *Semirelationship* isn't a term most women appreciate."

He grinned, relieved that he effectively had her endorsement of his strategy. "Give me credit, Kelly. Amber's made it crystal clear she doesn't want to get serious with anyone in racing, but I know she enjoys seeing me. A casual fling is the perfect solution for both of us."

ZACK SHOOK HANDS WITH yet another Getaway Resorts executive and counted the minutes until he could get out of the sponsor suite and down to his car. The action was always intense at the Bristol track. He needed to focus well ahead of the race.

Instead, not only was he pressing the flesh, his least favorite part of the job, but he was also constantly aware of Gaby, who was working the room. Since they'd agreed they were on hold until after Richmond, they'd kept their contact to the professional minimum. When he'd first met her, he'd have been thrilled at that. But now such distance only made Zack feel tense and frustrated, and he was barely hanging on to the techniques she'd taught him for bridging the gap with his family.

Zack headed to the bar for a glass of water, to keep up his prerace hydration. How could he feel he had Gaby's full support for his racing if they were barely talking? And what if they got to Richmond and she decided she didn't want to risk any kind of relationship? He gulped half a glass of water, then handed it back for a top-off. He needed to stop thinking about her until they were *off* hold.

"You look as if you just got a flat tire on the last lap." Brady came up behind Zack and thumped his shoulder lightly. He ordered a beer from the bartender along with a glass of wine, which he handed to Julie-Anne. He raised his glass to Zack. "Cheer up, son, you might even win."

Zack almost made a sarcastic retort. Then he remembered his charm school lessons and forced a grin that was meant to look easy. Somehow, it worked, took the edge off his irritation. Gaby sure knew what she was talking about when it came to changing his responses to his family.

Not thinking about her.

"The sponsor seems happy," Zack said to Julie-Anne, who

helped run the suite on race days. He was fond of his step-mother; she was crazy about Brady, and she'd always had a sympathetic spot for Zack, which set her apart from the rest of the world. Except Gaby.

Still not thinking about her.

"Some of these guys haven't been to a race before, so they're pretty excited…easy to please." Julie-Anne's dark eyes roamed the room and alighted on her daughter. "I hope Amber's okay. She's not big on crowds."

"She looks fine," Zack said mechanically. Did that guy in the orange polo shirt just *touch* Gaby?

Definitely not thinking about her.

"I hope we're done with her upsetting you," Brady said gruffly to Julie-Anne.

"*Gaby* upsets you?" Zack asked his stepmother, incredu-lous. Then realized from the surprised silence that they were talking about Amber. "Sorry, I mean, uh…"

Brady clapped him on the back with surprising bon-homie. "Don't worry, son, I can see you have some things on your mind."

Brady was right, who was Zack trying to kid?

Thinking about her. All the time.

ZACK LINED UP FOR THE race in sixth position, an excellent start, given he'd qualified early in the day on Thursday, when the track was still cold and the tires weren't sticking so easily.

Trent was beside him on the grid, in fifth. Though Zack managed to give his brother a casual wave as they circled the track ahead of the race, their proximity was freaking him out.

Get over it. Trent had as much right as him to this stretch of pavement. Now wasn't the time for Zack to get caught up in sibling rivalry. What would Gaby say?

Zack let thoughts of her take over, calm him. The next time he sensed Trent looking at him, he raised his hand in their old "good luck" signal from karting days, a circle made from his thumb and index finger. Evidently he had surprised Trent, because his brother fell back slightly, and in the scramble to hold his place in the lineup didn't get to respond.

They approached the start line; up ahead, the green flag waved. Then there was no time to think about anything other than the surge of forty-three engines and the jostling for early advantage.

Right from the start, Zack's car felt off. Even though it had performed well in qualifying, and after practice he'd told the guys the setup was perfect, it was too tight now. Which meant he risked driving straight into the wall on the corners. Zack cursed. Dave, his crew chief, spoke through his headset. "What's up?"

"No traction, we're too tight," Zack said as he wrestled the steering wheel just to stay in his groove through Turn Two. Trent had pulled ahead almost right away, and now Danny Cruise shot past him. Zack cursed again.

"We'll fix it when you pit," Dave said calmly.

The reassurance helped Zack, but it didn't do anything for the car. By the time he pitted on lap forty-nine, Zack had spoken to Chad over the headphones a couple of times, and he didn't sound happy.

Which riled Zack—did Chad think he was having a party out there?

The pit crew sprang into action, and although the stop wasn't short—fifteen point one seconds—the car felt a lot better afterward. When Zack relayed that to Dave, his crew chief gave a quiet harumph of relief. Then Chad came on the line and said, "Let's hope you can catch up to Trent."

"Thanks a lot," Zack muttered. Then reminded himself anyone who'd paid for a scanner at the track gates—and anyone in the media—could hear him. He added a pointless "Feeling good now" for their benefit. Gaby ought to be proud of him.

Gaby. Now there was a far more pleasant thought. One he'd better keep under control, he realized, as his spotter warned him Justin Murphy was coming up on his tail. Zack managed to block Murphy, and even pulled ahead a little. By the next pit stop, he'd regained a couple of places he'd lost. He wasn't exactly setting the track on fire, but if he could improve steadily, he might have a decent finish.

He knew it was wrong, but Zack couldn't help but take comfort from the fact Trent had fallen back, too. He was now sitting eighth, Zack eleventh. Plenty of time for both of them to move forward.

Zack soon moved up to tenth position by dint of an aggressive pass on Danny Cruise.

"Nice," Dave said. Sometimes, Zack wished he had a more excitable crew chief. But Dave was great at putting the car together, and that's what mattered.

Will Branch pulled on to the infield with smoke pouring from under his hood. Bad luck for Branch, good luck for Zack—it put him right on Trent's tail. Zack spent a couple of laps observing Trent's line. He noticed that his brother ran high each time he went into Turn Three. That was where Zack would pass him.

He began planning the move. "Gap," he told Mac, his spotter, instructing him to keep an eye on Trent and any opportunities to get by him.

"Roger that," Mac said. As spotter, he would also watch the cars coming up behind Zack, and would let him know if anything made the pass a bad idea.

Two laps later, Zack saw his chance. "Down," Mac said, telling him to go low around the pole line.

The flooring of the gas, the twist of the steering wheel, the change in air pressure as he slid past Trent all merged in a blur of action. When it ended, Zack was in front of his brother.

"Tail." A warning from Mac.

Dammit, Zack needed to keep his head in the game. No one got more fired up than Trent when someone passed him— he wasn't about to sit around and let Zack put distance between them. Zack checked his rearview mirror. Yep, Trent had moved up. Zack detected the faintest wobble in his brother's line, which signaled his impatience, and his intent to retaliate with a pass of his own.

"Number 448 low," Mac said.

Justin Murphy was trying to join the party. You never knew what Murphy would do next. Most of the time he was a responsible driver, but sometimes, it seemed some little devil took over and Justin pulled stunts that either won him the race or wiped out his rivals along with himself.

Zack managed to gain a few inches on Kent Grosso in front of him. Behind him, Trent hung on.

Then it happened.

Trent nudged Zack's bumper in the classic bump-and-pass move popular at the shorter tracks. The contact shunted Zack's car forward in the worst possible place for a too-tight car going into the turn.

Zack bit down on a curse and grappled to hold his line. The car scraped along the wall, producing a shower of friction sparks. Still, he hung on. Until another bump from Trent made it impossible.

Zack bounced off the wall and into his brother's car, sending Trent sideways, but not hard enough to do serious damage to Trent's car. The damage to Zack's car was already done. There was no crowd-pleasing spin out of control. Just a shredded tire and a walk to the infield for an ignominious end to his race.

Zack stuck his arm out the window to tell everyone he was okay. The he slumped forward until his helmet met the steering wheel. He wasn't okay. He'd just screwed up another race, thanks in large part to his brother, yet he knew damn well he'd be the one facing condemnation. The one person who might have sympathized was Gaby, but they were *on hold,* so he couldn't expect more than professional kindness. Damn.

Trent finished third. Zack strode to his brother's pit, right next to his own. He jumped over the wall, ready for when Trent got out of the car.

"You did that deliberately," he snarled as Trent removed his helmet.

Trent ran the back of his hand across his forehead, clammy after the long race. "Bump and pass, buddy. If the officials think I was out of line, they'll penalize me."

Zack suspected that wouldn't happen, unless someone kicked up a fuss.

"You can't stand me passing you," Zack said. "You've always got to be the center of attention, always the golden boy."

"Zack." Gaby arrived at the other side of the wall. "You okay?" A fine line creased her forehead. *Now* she wanted to know how he was, now that she was worried he might ruin his image in front of the reporter headed their way with a camera crew in tow.

"Fine," he growled.

"Just because you can't drive worth squat…" Trent raked his fingers through his hair. "Don't blame me if you can't keep your car in line."

"You're a jerk." Zack was making way more of a fuss than he would with any other driver. But this was personal, and he knew it.

"Snap out of it, Zack," Chad said. "You had a good race up until you crashed. Be satisfied with that."

Satisfied that his little brother had rammed him and was getting away scot-free? "I'm going to lodge a complaint," Zack said.

Chad's expression turned dark. Brady sucked air in through his teeth. Zack didn't care. He had no real intention of lodging a complaint against Trent—he would never do that to someone in his family—but it would be nice if someone just admitted that Trent had been in the wrong.

The reporter reached them. "Zack," he called, "was today's

accident history repeating itself? How do you feel about your brother's tactics?"

Brady's horrified expression mirrored Chad's.

"Zack," Gaby said calmly, reminding him to undo the damage now, rather than let it fester. Dammit, he felt like festering.

Part of him wanted to pull Gaby into his arms, to rest his chin on her head and draw strength from her. But she was the one who'd said they couldn't date.

He flung past her, past the reporter, and headed for his motor home alone.

CHAPTER FIFTEEN

AMBER PULLED UP OUTSIDE Brady's house—her mom's house, too, she reminded herself. She cut the engine, but didn't get out of the car right away.

It was one thing deciding she felt strong enough to confront her mom, quite another to actually do it. Amber tipped her head back against the seat and, eyes closed, took a deep breath.

As she'd said to Ryan at Bristol, there came a time when you had to think about why you were holding on to old baggage, and whether it was worth hanging on to at all. Especially if the weight of it stopped you from moving forward.

That's what she was here to find out, if that old baggage still meant anything.

She reached for the door handle. She could do this, without losing her temper and saying things she might regret. She wasn't the suspicious, angry person she'd been when she arrived back in Charlotte. The change, she had to admit, was partly due to Ryan. His sunny temperament lifted her out of her worries. His kisses reminded her of a side of herself she hadn't allowed out much. His admiration helped soothe the sting of rejection she'd felt for so long.

"Which means I can do this," she said aloud, and opened the car door.

Brady had said Amber must treat this place as her home, so she didn't knock, just went right in. She found her mom in the kitchen, peeling potatoes.

"Honey, how lovely to see you." Julie-Anne hugged her. Amber hugged back, but her mom felt the tension in her body.

"Is something wrong? Did Ryan do something?" Julie-Anne asked.

Amber shook her head, and once again considered chickening out.

"Are you sure?" Julie-Anne peered at her. "I could have Brady break his legs." She sounded as if she was only half-joking.

"Mom!" But it was nice to think of her mom protecting her. Maybe they could find a way to be close without ever discussing the past. "Brady wouldn't injure one of his own drivers," she said, trying to keep the conversation lighthearted.

"Too bad." Julie-Anne smiled, then added seriously, "Family comes first with Brady. If you need him to deal with Ryan…"

"Why didn't I come first with you?" Amber blurted.

Immediately, she wished she could take the words back. But there was no unsaying the question that had plagued her since she was twelve years old. When her mom had chosen her mean, drunk, cheating husband over her daughter.

Julie-Anne made a curious, high-pitched sound. "You said it. You finally said it." She took a step backward. "I always knew you thought it, but you shut me out whenever I tried to explain."

"I didn't want to hear excuses that I'd believe out of desperation, knowing in my heart they weren't true." Amber shivered; she chafed her upper arms with her hands. "Not when the facts spoke for themselves."

Julie-Anne's eyes filled with compassion. "Tell me," she invited. "Tell me the facts."

What, she didn't remember? Aware her legs wouldn't support her much longer, Amber sat down at the rustic pine kitchen table. She splayed her fingers on the surface and pressed hard. "First fact—you planned to leave Dad…we were going to live with Auntie Alice." Julie-Anne's sister in Los Angeles had offered to have them stay with her for as long as they needed to.

"Until we could get settled in a place of our own," Julie-Anne confirmed.

"Second fact—then Dad had his accident." Billy Blake had lost his job as a NASCAR Nationwide Series driver the moment his team owner realized what kind of man Billy was. Racing had been Billy's only incentive to stay sober—the accident happened while he was driving drunk on the interstate. He'd seriously injured another motorist and had been paralyzed from the waist down himself.

"I couldn't walk out on him while he was in hospital," Julie-Anne said. "That's fact three."

"Couldn't, wouldn't…" Amber saw hurt in her mom's eyes and steeled herself. "Fact four—so we stayed until Dad came home."

"It was September," her mom said. "Fact five is that school was about to start, and I thought you should go where we planned to be the rest of the year. No point spending a month at your old school, then being uprooted."

"Which leads us to fact six," Amber said. "You sent me away."

"Fact six," Julie-Anne corrected, "I sent you to Auntie Alice. The idea was, I would follow as soon as I could leave your father."

"Which took seven years," Amber said bitterly. "That's not a fact, that's abandonment." Even now, the knowledge that her mother had chosen to live with that jerk and had sent Amber away for seven long years made her shake with anger.

"If I'd had any idea," Julie-Anne began.

But Amber was beyond ifs, beyond facts. All that remained was hurt. "What?" she demanded. "You would have come sooner? I don't think so."

Julie-Anne's face was white. "I missed you so much, every single day."

"So much that you came to visit once a year, for two weeks."

"That was all the respite care I could afford," Julie-Anne said.

"A lot of NASCAR folk chipped in to help with your father's expenses—more than he deserved—but there was nothing left over. When it came to his day-to-day care, I was it."

"You must have realized, some time in those early days, that he wasn't going to get better." Amber paced the kitchen. "That you being there made no difference. But you stayed. You chose him over me."

Julie-Anne rubbed her face with her hands. "You think I should have walked out on a man who was paralyzed, then diagnosed with stomach cancer?"

"Yes, I think you should have walked out on the drunk who made your life and mine miserable. He didn't need a wife, Mom, he needed someone to humiliate." Amber's eyes filled with tears. "*I* needed *you*. My mother." Her aunt had been kind, welcoming…but it was hard living in someone else's house through those teenage years filled with change and confusion and pain.

"Sweetheart, I missed you every minute of every day," Julie-Anne said.

Amber snorted, though she wanted desperately to believe. "If you'd come to L.A., surely social services would have provided assistance—they wouldn't have left Billy on his own. Were you…were you afraid to leave?"

Julie-Anne had been afraid of Billy when he was healthy. Not that he would hit her—for all his faults, he'd never done that—but of his mean temper, his bullying ways.

Her mother shook her head. "By that stage he was too pathetic for me to be frightened of. He was so weak, there were days when I thought about putting a pillow over his face and ending it."

Amber gasped.

Her mother smiled grimly. "I would never have done it. But believe me, revenge for those years that he'd cheated on me and deprived you of a normal childhood would have been sweet."

"You didn't have to kill him," Amber said awkwardly. "You just had to walk out the door."

"It's not that easy." Julie-Anne shook her head, remembering. "If you have any kind of code of honor that you live by…well, let's just say my code didn't include walking out on someone in such desperate circumstances."

"I could understand—" Amber ignored the flare of hope in her mom's eyes "—if you hadn't had me."

"I came to see you for Christmas," her mom said. "On that first visit, when you met me at the airport, my heart just about exploded. I knew there was no way I could do it—I couldn't stay with your father another minute."

Amber's eyes stung. "What changed your mind?"

"You were bright, cheerful," Julie-Anne said. "You were putting on a brave face so I wouldn't be worried."

Amber hadn't realized she was that transparent.

"But beneath…beneath your missing me, which I could tell you did," Julie-Anne said, "there was a genuine…peace. I hadn't seen that in you before."

"Our home wasn't a peaceful place," Amber agreed. "But I didn't blame you for that."

"Seeing you without those shadows under your eyes that I'd always thought were just a part of your face…" Julie-Anne swallowed. "The guilt that we'd stayed with your father for so long…" Her voice broke, and she pressed a fist to her mouth.

"I didn't mind, as long as you and I were together." Amber pressed her fingers to the corners of her eyes, where tears welled.

"You should have minded," Julie-Anne said fiercely. "You should have hated me for raising you in that environment."

"I didn't hate you…before you sent me away." Amber was well aware of the implication of her words. But it was true—she had hated her mother through much of their time apart. On good days, the hate had mellowed to hurt and anger. "But I did hate *him*."

"I'm not going to tell you he was a decent person," Julie-Anne said. "He had a rough upbringing, but when he discovered motor racing…well, I thought it might be the saving of him."

"You couldn't save him," Amber said brutally.

"No—" her mother's voice steadied "—and it takes more than driving a race car to save a man's soul I know." She sighed. "After you went to Alice, I kept thinking, *It won't be long now. Another month, or two.* But that first year, dealing with the insurance company, having the house modified for your dad's wheelchair, handling the sympathy that came pouring in…it passed in the blink of an eye."

Not for Amber, but she didn't point that out.

"I kept thinking he'd get to a stage where he was independent enough for me to leave. Then when they diagnosed the cancer…"

"Two years later," Amber reminded her.

After a hesitation, Julie-Anne nodded. "Then I thought, he's going. I'll hang around until he's gone." Her eyes turned pleading. "No one should have to die alone."

Amber didn't want to get a glimpse of her mom's dilemma. The fact was, her dad had remained relatively healthy for most of those years. After the house had been modified, he could have lived independently. And he'd had friends. Drinking buddies.

"I wanted—" Amber choked on her words "—I thought about…hurting myself, just to make you come to me."

Julie-Anne let out a sob. "Don't say that."

"I couldn't do it," Amber said. "I was afraid you still might not come, even if I was hurt and I…I wasn't brave enough to face that."

Tears streamed down her mother's face.

"Amber, my darling." Julie-Anne reached for her; Amber shrank away. "I'm so sorry. I can tell you as best I can why I made the decisions I did. But I know I can't satisfy you. I can't even satisfy myself." Julie-Anne twisted her hands together. "Forgive me. Please, darling, forgive me."

Amber's throat clogged, she couldn't speak. But her instincts screamed *No*.

Julie-Anne gazed at the tiled floor and said quietly, "Your

forgiveness, or lack of it, doesn't change the fact that I love you so much it keeps me awake at nights worrying about you. Although I have Brady, who is a wonderful man and I love him to bits, there's an Amber-shaped space in my heart. Nobody else can fill it, no one ever will."

It was too much. Amber wanted more than anything to believe…but she couldn't wipe out those lonely teenage years, the consuming jealousy of her father… She found herself taking great gulps of air, and clapped a hand over her mouth.

When she could speak, she said shakily, "I appreciate you telling me how it was. I know things weren't easy for you."

Julie-Anne's eyes lit with hope, and she stretched out a hand.

"I'm sorry, Mom, it's not enough."

Stricken, Julie-Anne swayed; her hand dropped. Amber felt like a jerk. But she'd told the truth.

As she left the kitchen and walked swiftly toward the front door, she berated herself. She shouldn't have come back to Charlotte. There was no way through this.

I need to talk to Ryan.

It was a crazy thought, a couple of kisses didn't make her his girlfriend. He'd probably run a mile if she tried to tell him her woes.

Yet she wanted to take the risk. *Right now.*

She hit the front porch at a run…then came to a halt when she saw Brady pull up in his classic Mustang.

Oh, hell. Now Brady would go inside and find Julie-Anne in tears and that would be the end of any relationship he and Amber might have had.

"Hey, Amber." Brady's greeting was hearty. "That was some weekend, huh?"

With Trent finishing third, and Ryan having his first win, it had indeed been a great weekend for Matheson Racing, if you overlooked Zack's DNF.

"It was great," she said, surprised how unsettling the thought of ruining her fledgling relationship with Brady was.

"Like I told Chad, I always knew Ryan had what it takes," Brady said with satisfaction.

Amber made some noncommittal noise and wondered if it was best to jump straight in her car and drive, or to warn Brady that she and her mom had argued.

"I hope you didn't mind me sticking my oar in when he came to the motor home, but I was worried he was up to his old tricks when I saw him making eyes at you," Brady said.

It took her a second to click that he was still talking about Ryan. "His old tricks?" she asked, still distracted by thoughts of her mom.

"Girls," Brady said darkly. "That guy has—" He cut off abruptly. "You're not serious about him, are you?"

"No," Amber said, unsure if it was true or not. "Brady, there's something I should—"

"Good, that's good." Brady scratched his head. "Ryan dated so many women last season he could have put a revolving door on his motor home."

Amber felt suddenly sick. "Really?"

Brady must have sensed her reaction. "I'm not saying he slept with them all," he said hastily.

It sure sounded like he had.

"Jeff, his dad, gave him the hard word," Brady said approvingly. "Told him the girls had to go."

If Amber knew one thing about Ryan, it was that he wanted to please his father.

"Ryan's been a monk ever since," Brady said. "That's why I got such a surprise to see him with you."

"We're just friends." It was a lie. Because now, it felt as if she and Ryan were nothing. She wasn't sure what was worse. That Ryan had implied she'd misjudged him with her accusations that he was a womanizer, that he'd allowed trust to build between them, or that he'd willingly ended his relationships just because his father asked him to.

He'd better not be seeing her as the first in a new wave of

revolving-door girlfriends. Before he got to kiss her again, she would ask Ryan some tough questions. He'd better have the right answers.

GABY SLIPPED IN TO Matheson Racing on Tuesday morning hopeful she wouldn't run into Zack. Best if she carried out her mission without seeing him.

Because this couldn't go on. They'd come so close to a media disaster at Bristol, and it wouldn't have been entirely Zack's fault, though doubtless he'd have gotten the blame. The whole Matheson family needed a major readjustment of their attitude. If things didn't change soon, Zack would either bomb out in making the Chase, or he'd lose it in public. Neither of those would make Getaway, or Sandra, happy.

Most importantly, neither of them would make Zack happy.

Gaby shoved the thought aside. She had enough reasons for this meeting without letting it get personal.

"Is Chad around?" she asked Amber, whose manner was unusually subdued.

"Brady went upstairs to see him a few minutes ago," Amber said.

Great, Gaby could tackle Zack's father and brother in one swoop.

Upstairs, she saw Brady talking to Chad through the glass wall of Chad's office. Neither man looked happy. What she had to say wouldn't make them any happier…but that was too bad. She knocked on the door and entered.

"Gaby." Chad wiped away his somber expression and replaced it with a smile of genuine friendship. She was counting on that friendship to get her through the next few minutes. "Could we talk later? Dad and I are in the middle of—"

"I wanted to see both of you," she said. "It's important."

"About Zack." Brady stated the obvious. Both men eyed her expectantly—she took it as a positive sign that they were willing to suspend whatever they'd been discussing to focus on Zack.

"This thing between Zack and Trent—" she decided to start with Trent, since he wasn't here to take offence "—is hurting Zack's racing. There must be some way you—we—can smooth things over between them."

Chad frowned. "I spend half my working life trying to keep those two from each other's throats."

"Well, it's not working," Gaby said. Chad raised his eyebrows at her bluntness. "Trent was out of line at Bristol, and you know it."

"So was Zack," Chad said. "That garbage about lodging a complaint…"

"Unless you can wipe Zack's memory, nothing will change," Brady opined. "He's got it fixed in his head that Trent deliberately put him out of the Chase four years ago and nothing will shift it."

"Maybe he's right," Gaby said.

Brady bristled. "It was an accident, the kind that happens in racing all the time. Unavoidable."

"I know Zack didn't react well last weekend, and it wasn't the first time," Gaby argued. "But let's say you're right, let's say the problem lies entirely with Zack…"

"Let's say it does." Zack's voice came from behind her. "After all, that's what everyone thinks."

CHAPTER SIXTEEN

OH, HECK. HEART IN her mouth, Gaby spun to face him. "Zack..."

"Hello, Gaby." His tone was pleasant, but his eyes were furious. "What a surprise to find you here."

"I wanted to talk to your dad and Chad—"

"Behind my back," he completed.

"Calm down, Zack." Chad said exactly the wrong words, as he so often did.

"Maybe you all would like me to step out of the room so you can go on talking about me," Zack suggested.

"This meeting was my idea, not theirs." Gaby didn't want to damage his fragile relationships any further. "Someone has to face up to the fact that your past with Trent is affecting your racing...."

"Do *you* believe me when I tell you Trent rammed me deliberately back then?"

"I—I didn't see the race," she prevaricated.

He dipped his head, and when he raised it again his features were set in stone. "You're no different from these guys." He dismissed Brady and Chad with a jerk of his head. "You think I'm holding a needless grudge. That the crash was purely an accident, and that I'm the one holding myself back."

"I don't know," she said honestly. "I don't care. Whatever happened, you need to get past this fixation with Trent so you can win more races."

Zack stiffened at her use of the word *fixation.* As a PR professional, she knew that she should have chosen more carefully, but as a woman who cared about him, frustration was getting the better of her.

"What I need," Zack said, "is people around me that I can trust. People who give me their full support."

"You can trust us," Brady said gruffly. "Hell, if you didn't have our full support, do you think we'd put you behind the wheel of a stock car? And if you *don't* trust us—"

"Of course he does." Gaby jumped in to prevent the inevitable meltdown. "But I agree with Zack, you don't show him anywhere near as much support as you show Trent."

Zack rounded on her, furious. "I was talking about *you*."

She ignored the stab of pain—he was pointing the finger at her because he was afraid to rock the boat further with his family. That's what she told herself, at least.

She could deal with Zack later. Right now, it was important to get her message across to Chad and Brady. "I know Trent's a brilliant driver—"

Beside her, Zack made a sound of hurt disbelief. She steeled herself to continue. "But you guys act as if he's the only driver that counts on this team. If there's any dispute between him and Zack, you always defer to Trent."

"This isn't a school playground," Brady blustered. "They're grown men, they can fight their own battles."

"And grown men—fathers and brothers—should know better than to take sides," she shot back.

"Dammit, Gaby, shut up," Zack snapped.

She wheeled on him. "I won't shut up. You need to deal with your family's hostility toward you, their intolerance—" she ignored Brady's growl "—or you'll wind up racing even worse than you are now."

"It's not all about the racing," Zack roared.

His words fell into a shocked silence. By Matheson standards, he'd just committed sacrilege.

"Then what is it about?" Brady asked, bewildered.

Gaby couldn't believe Zack had finally admitted what mattered most. His jaw locked tight; he wasn't about to answer.

"It's about family," she said. "You guys need to stop treating Zack like a second-class citizen."

Zack clutched his head. "Can't you see you're making things worse? When I said you could run a PR campaign with my family—" frantically, she signaled him to stop talking, but he was oblivious "—I didn't mean you could attack them, or betray my confidence."

Chad jumped in. "What do you mean, Gaby's running a PR campaign with your family?"

"Yeah, what the hell is that?" Brady demanded.

Zack smacked his forehead. His shoulders sagged.

"I can explain," Gaby began.

Zack didn't let her. "Gaby offered to help me mend my fences with you if I put more effort into the bachelor contest. She's helped me talk to you, find the right words. Back away from arguments."

"You mean, this whole Mr. Reasonable thing you've been doing is an act?" Chad demanded.

"Not an act," Gaby said. "Just planning his communications better, to prevent the crossed wires your family excels at."

"A publicity stunt," Brady said, disgusted. "I suppose when you told Amber I'm inspiring, that was part of it."

"No, Dad, it wasn't," Zack said.

"Well, it worked," Brady said grimly. "Had me thinking you were a regular prodigal son, back in the fold."

"When you invited me out for a beer the other night," Chad said. "Was that part of it, too?"

"No, dammit," Zack said, frustrated. "Well, yeah, I guess. You'll remember you didn't accept my invitation, which shouldn't have surprised me."

Gaby closed her eyes. He was too honest for his own good, something she'd never thought she'd say about a man.

Chad slammed his hand down on his desk. "I can't believe you. You say you want back on the team, so we give it to you. I bust my butt finding you a sponsor—"

"Like that was so painful," Gaby retorted. "You got your wife back in the process, you should be thanking Zack."

A strangled sound came from Zack. Chad ignored her and continued on. "I've been so busy keeping you and Trent from each other's throats that it's taken me months to notice there's something weird going on with the team's finances—"

"What do you mean?" Zack demanded.

"Forget it, Dad and I are working it out with Tony Winters."

"You see," Gaby said. "That's a classic example of how you shut Zack out of family business. If Trent had asked that question, you'd have answered."

Chad shot her a look that suggested if he'd ever liked her in the least, he no longer did. "And now it turns out you're playing us," he said to Zack, "with the help of this scheming, manipulative…" He waved at Gaby.

Zack took a step forward. "Take that back, right now."

The menace in his voice was unmistakable. Gaby's heart swelled. Even though he was hopping mad, Zack was defending her.

Unlike Zack, Chad didn't allow himself to get distracted, he knew where the real argument was. He said a perfunctory, "Sorry, Gaby."

The apology robbed Zack of ammunition and left Chad in control of the moral high ground. "Zack, you're seriously screwed up in your attitude to this family and this team," he said. "You need to think about how much you want to be a part of it and whether or not you're willing to quit playing games and conduct yourself like a real Matheson."

The flicker in his eyes said he knew his words had to have hurt, and he regretted them. Gaby would bet that if Brianna was here, Chad would have moderated his reaction. Instead, he held his ground. Brady moved alongside his oldest son, and with the two of them joined in glaring solidarity, even Gaby conceded Zack didn't stand a chance.

But unlike previous occasions, where she'd told him to be the bigger man and back down from a fight, she didn't want him to do that now. Unlike those other times, this was important—huge. Zack was in the right, darn it.

He swallowed, and she hoped it wasn't his pride. Right now, she was proud of Zack Matheson and she wanted him to be proud of himself, too.

"As for you," Chad said to her, "you can count on me talking to Sandra about your little games. She needs to know just how unprofessional you are."

There went her promotion—no way would Sandra see a "family PR campaign" as being in Motor Media's best interests. Gaby felt sick, but she defiantly answered, "I'd expect nothing else from you. To you, Zack and this whole conflict are just a part of the business, not a part of the family."

Through gritted teeth, Zack said, "Leave Sandra out of this, Chad. Leave Gaby out."

He was protecting her again. It took Gaby's breath away... and what came flooding in to replace it was a surge of... *Love.*

I love him.

She didn't even try to deny it. She was an idiot not to have realized it sooner. She'd fallen in love with the prickliest man in the world. A guy with a chip on his shoulder and a natural tendency for screwing up relationships.

A guy who cared so much about his relationships that he'd returned to Charlotte and willingly become the least regarded person on the team, just so he could get closer to his family, she reminded herself. Who'd let Gaby blackmail him into working hard on the bachelor contest in exchange for her help in repairing the family rift. Who got out there every weekend and raced, even when he felt he didn't have the respect of his team, or any chance of winning. Yet he drove his heart out regardless.

Who every time he got hurt, fought the urge to retreat, and kept putting himself out there. Who right now was protecting her, even though he was mad with her.

Who *wouldn't* fall in love with Zack Matheson?

"I'll talk to Sandra if I damn well want," Chad said. "I've had enough of your games, both of you. Sometimes I wish I could fire you, Zack."

"I can't do this," Zack said. Gaby didn't know if he meant continue the argument, tolerate his family's attitude, or be a part of the team.

He headed for the door, shoulders straight and stiff. He paused, one hand on the handle, and turned back to Gaby. "I trusted you," he said. "I thought we had something."

"Zack, please…"

"It's over. Everything's over."

He left, and Gaby's heart went with him. For a long moment, silence seethed. Then Chad said, "You can get out, too."

Gaby stalked out of the office, head held high, but waited a couple of minutes before going outside. She didn't want to see Zack. When she got into her car, she locked the doors and cried until she'd soaked through every tissue in her purse.

How could she have misjudged this situation so badly? Knowing what a deep thinker Zack was, how willing he was to accept responsibility for his share of the rift in his family and to work to fix it, she'd assumed the other guys would have the same attitude. That they just needed someone to set them on the right track. Turned out Zack was a bigger man than any of them. Now, she'd screwed up the work they'd done with the Mathesons, screwed up her promotion and screwed up any hope that Zack might return her feelings.

At last, she exhausted her tears. Gaby balled up the sodden mess of tissues, stuffed them into the cupholder. And wondered how long it would take Sandra to fire her.

"YOU GOING OUT?" Jeff Thorne asked.

The question reminded Ryan why moving back in with his parents hadn't been his best idea.

"I'm picking he has a date." Terence Thorne, Ryan's grandfather, weighed in.

Oh, yeah, and somehow Granddad got to say his piece, too, even though he was as much a guest around here as Ryan, having moved in at the same time.

"A date?" Jeff asked.

Ryan wondered why he was even in this conversation, since his father and grandfather were quite capable of carrying it on without him.

"On a Wednesday night?" Jeff continued, brows angled upward.

"I know what night it is," Ryan assured him.

"You leave for Montreal tomorrow, don't you?" Granddad asked.

No, Granddad, they changed the whole schedule just so I can go out Wednesday nights. "I won't be late," he said. Not that he owed them an explanation, but it might shut them up.

"You seeing Amber Blake again?" Jeff sounded carefully neutral. He liked that Amber had a NASCAR background, liked her connection to Matheson Racing, and genuinely liked Julie-Anne. But he'd heard rumors Amber's attitude to the sport wasn't as reverent as he thought everyone's should be.

"I'm having a drink with her, Dad," Ryan said patiently. Sometimes he wished he hadn't been brought up so respectful toward his elders. It would be much easier if he could say, "Butt out," and leave. Instead he said, "It's not a big deal."

No, the big deal—the big night would be after this Sunday's race, he'd decided. He would make love to Amber, convince her to stay on in Montreal for a day's sightseeing. Get a serious start on that fling Kelly had recommended he have.

Maybe not recommended, exactly, he conceded, but definitely endorsed. Just the thought of seeing Amber improved his mood; he smiled at his dad.

Reassured, Jeff smiled back. "You're a good kid, Ryan. I know you won't forget what matters."

Racing. Winning the NASCAR Nationwide Series. Like his father had and his grandfather before him. That was what mattered, and Ryan wasn't about to argue. He said goodbye to his folks, gave every appearance of listening to their advice about alcohol consumption and the benefits of an early night for a NASCAR driver, then headed out to his Mustang convertible.

Amber—ever-independent Amber—had insisted she meet Ryan at the bar in uptown Charlotte where they planned to have a drink, rather than have him pick her up. She'd sounded noncommittal on the phone, but he was used to her vagaries.

After next weekend, when she would officially be his girlfriend, in a no-strings way, he'd expect to pick her up from her place. Thankfully she wasn't staying with Brady, she was living in Julie-Anne's house in NoDa, the Bohemian area of Charlotte. At least one of them needed a private space.

He walked into the bar and saw Amber right away. She didn't look happy that he was late. Ryan kissed her lips briefly, enjoying the challenge of getting in and out of the embrace before she fired off one of her shots. Mmm, she tasted good, even in that brief moment.

"You look great," he said after ordering a couple of beers for them. She wore white jeans and a flowing green halter top with two layers, the top one a sexy, gauzy fabric.

Her smile had an edge to it, but he'd given up on trying to read Amber's mind, so he gave her an easy smile back. "Sorry I'm late. I had to listen to a few lectures from Dad and Granddad about taking my job seriously."

"Maybe you should get your own place."

Ryan's pulse thudded. Did she mean she wanted to be alone with him? The beers arrived, he passed one to Amber.

"I probably should. But being with Mom and Dad is convenient. Listening to the odd lecture is a small price to pay."

Though lately, it had felt like more of a burden. These days, whenever his Dad or Granddad launched into their spiel about the duties of a NASCAR driver, Ryan felt increasingly as if his racing career was part of a long Thorne tradition that he'd been raised to fulfill rather than something he wanted to do for himself.

He took a long swig of his beer. "I love NASCAR, there's nothing else I want to do."

Amber blinked. "Where did that come from?"

He gave his head a sharp shake to clear it. "Sorry, just thinking aloud." When she didn't move on, he said, "I was thinking that this year, I've been feeling kind of tied down by my racing."

"Is that so bad? You *should* feel tied to what you love," she said.

Ryan shrugged. Was she talking about racing or him and her? Because they definitely weren't at the *love* stage. He kept it casual and said, "You're right, Dad would say racing is all about driving but it's also all about meeting expectations. Your team's, your sponsors', your fans'." He thought about that. "I have to admit, sometimes I wonder where the passion fits into all that."

"Surely passion dictates the choices you make."

"I guess," he said.

"Or maybe you're a guy who doesn't make a lot of conscious choices. Maybe you go with the flow." Amber's eyes were unreadable as she sipped her beer. Had she meant that last comment as an insult?

Man, she could be hard work. Ryan sighed. Maybe he should find someone less complicated for his fling. Then he looked at her mouth, heard the musical tones of her voice and knew that, for a while at least, it had to be this woman.

AMBER WAS DRINKING HER beer way too fast, fortifying herself to ask Ryan exactly what he was up to.

Maybe he was on the level. By Brady's own admission, Ryan had behaved himself this season. At his age he'd be maturing every year...and everyone had things in their past they weren't proud of. If he'd changed... She realized how much she wanted him to have changed. Her head buzzed.

"Passion is the opposite of opportunism," she said. "If there's something you really want, you'll make the right choices, and you won't let obstacles stand in your way."

Unlike Julie-Anne, who had allowed obstacles to keep her and Amber apart. *Don't go there. It's too hard.* She hadn't seen her mom since their argument, and Brady's manner when he'd run in to her at team headquarters had been cool. She'd seen in his clamped jaw the desire to berate her, but she guessed Julie-Anne had forbidden him to interfere.

Amber forced a smile at Ryan. "And if you're following your passion, being tied down would feel good."

He reached across the table and held her hand. "You older women are pretty smart."

She shivered as his thumb found her pulse and caressed the spot in lazy circles. He was so darned sexy, she could scarcely think.

Ask him now. Before you chicken out.

"Ryan..." She clutched his fingers. "What do you want from me?"

"What do I want?" His blue eyes darkened to cobalt as his gaze wandered her face, her shoulders. A wave of intense heat swept Amber.

"I want you to have dinner with me after qualifying in Montreal," he said. "A serious dinner, where we get dressed up and I pick you up from your hotel."

It wasn't quite what she'd expected, but it was a start. "Dinner might be a possibility," she said. She wanted to ask, *What else?*

He picked up on her expectancy; he grinned, and leaned

forward across the table. "Maybe I should tell you that I have more than just dinner in mind."

She drew in a breath as he ran his thumb over her knuckles.

"After dinner in Montreal," he said, "I want you in my arms. I want to make love with you."

"I—me, too," she said, flustered at his bluntness even though it mirrored her own style.

"You make me feel free." He grinned. "And easy."

Free was good. Easy…not so good. It wasn't exactly the word she'd hoped to hear in the context of increased intimacy with him. Amber drew back, but Ryan held fast to her hand. She let out a calming breath and said, "But I don't want either of us to go into this with the wrong expectations."

"I totally respect you for saying that," he said.

He did?

"Believe me, sweetheart, we're on the same page." Ryan brought her hand to his mouth and nipped her knuckle. Desire shot through Amber, the sensation so strong, she almost dissolved. "We'll make love soon," he said and she almost screamed with frustration that it wasn't going to happen *right now*. "No strings," he promised. "I won't hold you to anything."

No…strings? An alarm clanged inside Amber. "What do you mean?"

He nipped another knuckle. Somehow, she forced herself to concentrate. "I respect that you don't want to get seriously involved with anyone in NASCAR." He laughed. "Hell, sometimes I think it's the smartest thing I've ever heard. I'm the same, I don't want a serious involvement."

"With someone in NASCAR?" she asked, confused.

"With anyone. That's why we'll be perfect together."

Perfect flew out the window, to be replaced with *secondrate. Shoddy.* Amber felt as if her heart was being squeezed all over again, just has it had been when she'd argued with her mom. "Let me get this straight. You're suggesting we have sex—" she wasn't about to dignify his suggestion by calling it making love "—but we won't be involved?"

"Don't think I'm suggesting a one-night stand," he said, picking up on her tone. "No way."

"A two-night stand?" she asked.

His eyes narrowed. "I want to make love with you. More than once. A lot. I know you want it, too."

"What if I tell you I want involvement?" she said. "A real relationship?" His grasp on her hand slackened, and she withdrew it.

Ryan took a considered swig of his beer. "I would say this is a new development, given you said you don't date NASCAR guys." He sounded aggrieved, as if she was changing the rules on him and it wasn't fair.

Anger exploded inside her, forced Amber to her feet. "Here's a newsflash for you, buster. NASCAR or no NASCAR, I have *always* wanted a man I can trust and depend on. A man I can love."

Her outburst was so far outside the realm of his expectations that she'd silenced him.

He groped for words. "But your thing about NASCAR…"

"I don't have a thing about NASCAR," she snapped, and realized that although she might have in the past, she was beyond that now. "I have a thing about guys who think women should be grateful for the opportunity to sleep with them, who think they're so all-fired special that the rules of human decency don't apply to them."

She was aware of people at neighboring tables staring at them, but Ryan's gaze didn't move from hers. Amber balled her fists. "I'm not dumb enough to fall for a jerk like my father."

It was the ultimate insult, and he realized it, going by the way his face paled.

"Hey." His fingers circled her wrist, he tugged her back into her chair. "Before you get hung up on making comparisons with your dad, let me point out that I never for one moment led you to believe I wanted a serious girlfriend. You know racing is my priority, and that I keep relationships somewhere near the surface. Hell, I'm not proud of that, I don't think any woman is particularly lucky to have me. But I want you, you want me—I still don't see the harm."

Before she could even begin the mammoth task of setting him straight, he continued, "There's a bigger picture here, but I guess I'm the only one looking at it. I have a dream to pursue, one that's damned hard, one that a thousand other guys are waiting to snatch if I don't grab it with both hands."

"All right then, here's what I see when I look at the bigger picture." She leaned across the table. "I see a guy who thinks passion is an invitation to dinner and a roll in the hay." Her voice filled with contempt, as much for her own naiveté.

"You don't know the first thing about passion," she said. "You race a fast car, but the way you're doing it has nothing to do with passion. Think about why you get behind that wheel each week—because it sure as heck isn't for yourself."

Color rose from Ryan's neck, suffused his face. "Lady, you are way off. You have no idea what you're talking about."

Amber stood, and this time he made no move to stop her. "Grow up, Ryan."

She stalked out of the bar. Fury carried her as far as the door. Outrage propelled her to her car. Pain had her hunched over her steering wheel, sobbing for something she'd thought she had, but that for her might never exist.

CHAPTER SEVENTEEN

ZACK KEPT TO HIMSELF at Atlanta. He didn't have much say in the matter, given he wasn't talking to Gaby, and his family wasn't talking to him. He confined his conversation to Dave and the rest of the crew. He'd help get the car right, even if everything else was screwed up to hell and back.

I knew all along that my focus had to be on my racing, he chided himself as he sat in the hauler flicking through the folder of press clippings Gaby had sent over. He'd let himself get distracted by the need to build bridges with his family—big mistake. The only way to do that was to win races.

And he'd let himself get distracted by his feelings for Gaby. An even bigger mistake. Just thinking her name made his heart twist. Dammit, he'd trusted her. When he'd walked into the office at the front of the hauler and found her plotting with his dad and brother, found her suggesting the problems between them were all his fault...he couldn't remember the last time something hurt so much.

He paused in his scanning to read an article from one of the women's magazines. The headline: *Zack Wows American Women.* Garbage. Moving on, he found one titled *We Love Zack.* He sighed. The few headlines from the sports media had a very different tone. One respected paper had summed it up with a pithy *The Shortest Comeback in History?*

Dammit, how was he supposed to win races when he had to spend half his time on the bachelor contest? Hours spent schmoozing with journalists and fans, while his rivals—his brother—improved their fitness, or replayed old races to learn from their mistakes.

"How're you doing?" Brady's gruff voice interrupted Zack's thoughts. His dad stepped up behind him.

Zack kept his eyes on the clippings. "Fine."

Brady cleared his throat. "Good qualifying."

Zack's qualifying position—fifteenth—was nearer to okay than good, but he didn't call his dad on that. He grunted his thanks.

"That meeting the other day," Brady began awkwardly.

No way did Zack want to talk about that right now, not when he was getting his head into race space. "Dad, I get that you're mad with me…"

He felt a brief touch of Brady's hand on his shoulder, then it was gone. Absurdly, Zack felt moisture behind his eyes.

"Not mad," Brady said.

Zack closed the folder.

"More…sad," Brady admitted reluctantly. "That this is where we ended up." He held Zack's gaze.

"Yeah," Zack said. "Me, too." He waited for his father to suggest a way out of this mess. To say that things didn't always have to be this way.

Brady didn't say anything.

"How are you getting along with Amber?" Zack asked.

Brady grimaced. "I like her, though she's giving Julie-Anne enough grief for ten daughters."

Zack wondered if his dad *liked* him. Loved him, yes. But like…

Brady cleared his throat. "Well." He jerked a nod at the press clippings. "Guess I'd better leave you to your work."

Something inside Zack shriveled and withered. Things would always be this way, he realized. They would never get any better. He'd been naive to imagine they could. He swallowed. "Yeah."

He opened the folder.

"Gaby…" Brady said awkwardly.

Zack didn't look up. "What about her?"

"She cares a lot about you," Brady said. "She took a risk coming to see me and Chad."

"She betrayed my confidence."

Brady grabbed the folder from the table, startling Zack. "Dad?"

Brady puffed out his cheeks. "We might not be much good at this family stuff, but maybe you could do things differently with her."

As if Gaby was some kind of consolation prize.

"Things aren't so hot between us right now," Zack said.

"I get the feeling she'd do anything for you. That's a big deal." Brady dropped the folder back on the table.

As his father left, his words replayed through Zack's head. He was surprised to find a tendril of hope unfurling.

Of all the things he'd lost in the past few days, the loss of Gaby hurt the most. If his dad was right…his pulse quickened at the thought. Maybe he'd been too hard on her. Maybe he should find out whose side she was really on.

GABY KEPT WAITING FOR Sandra to mention that Chad had complained about Gaby's conduct. When her boss said nothing, Gaby could only conclude Chad hadn't said anything. Yet.

She and Sandra had watched the Atlanta race from the Taney Motorsports hospitality suite. Zack had finished fifth, which meant he had a real, though far from certain, chance at making the Chase for the NASCAR Sprint Cup.

"How did Zack end up with eight column inches in this paper, when my client, who happened to win the race, only got five?" Sandra grumbled good-naturedly. She dropped the Charlotte newspaper on Gaby's desk. "Good job."

"Good enough to get me promoted?" Gaby said automatically. Richmond, and Sandra's decision, was just a week away.

"Quite possibly." Sandra patted Gaby on the shoulder—maternal gestures seemed to come naturally to her these days—then left to talk to Kylie.

Gaby processed Sandra's words every which way and came to the same conclusion every time: she wasn't just a contender for the job, she was a *strong* contender. As long as Chad didn't blab to Sandra—perhaps he'd decided he didn't come out of it looking too good himself so it was, therefore, best to keep quiet—the security Gaby longed for was within her grasp.

She should be ecstatic. But instead of bubbles of euphoria, there was only a quiet trickle of relief, and the fizz in the pit of her stomach was decidedly flat.

I miss Zack.

"Hi," Zack said from her doorway.

She squawked, waking up a cloud of butterflies somewhere inside her. "I was just—what are you doing here?"

He closed the door behind him and came to perch on the edge of her desk. "Apologizing."

"Oh." She drew back in surprise.

"You need to watch those one-syllable words," he warned her.

"Sorry," she said automatically.

"Now you're stealing my word," he chided.

Gaby shook her head, bemused. What did he have to be so lighthearted about?

"I'm sorry I overreacted when I overheard you talking to my father and Chad," he said. "I was a jerk."

Gaby pulled her thoughts together. "I shouldn't have barged in without consulting you first. I just got riled up."

"On my behalf." His voice held a tender note that made her heart seize.

She nodded. "You've put so much work into your family, it's time they did their share."

"You're starting to sound like me," he said, amused.

She groaned. "Shoot me now."

Chuckling, Zack came around to her side of the desk.

When he held out his hands, Gaby let him pull her to her feet. "I missed you," he murmured, very close to her lips.

"Me, too," she breathed, one eye on the door of her office. At least she knew that Motor Media staff were polite enough to knock when they encountered a closed door....

Then he kissed her.

It was like coming home, Gaby thought, as she wrapped her arms around Zack, pressed her body to his. His wonderful, strong hands holding her, his mouth exploring, seeking, finding. The buildup of unmistakable heat. *Oh, yes, I want this. Forever.*

She put all her love into the kiss, gave to him from the deepest part of her soul. The embrace then took on a new urgency, his caresses grew more intimate. When they broke apart, Zack ran a shaky hand through his hair.

"Wow," he said. Gaby nodded; she couldn't trust herself to speak. He wrapped his arms around her again, loosely this time, and rested his chin on her head. "Gaby..."

"Mmm?"

"Thanks for being on my side through all this."

She pulled away to look up at him. "Of course I'm on your side."

He dropped a kiss on her nose. "I know things are at an impasse with Dad and the guys just now, but I couldn't have gotten as far as I have the past few weeks without you."

Gaby blinked away sudden emotion.

"Surprisingly enough I think I can get my head clear enough of all the crap that's been going on, and race well at Richmond."

"If there's anything I can do to help," she said eagerly.

He paused. "As a matter of fact..."

"What is it?"

"There are two bachelor events in Richmond," he said.

"The televised reader party and the interview with Olivia Winton," she agreed.

"It's on race day," he said. "The interview."

She grimaced. "I know, it's a pain. But Olivia's the most popular breakfast host in America." She wrapped her arms around his waist. "That interview could mean the difference between winning and losing the Bachelor of the Year. The organizers expect most viewers to text their votes Friday night, after the reader party. The interview next morning will give them a chance to vote again, and will pick up any stragglers."

"I just don't see how I can attend those events and still race well," he said. "The two races I've had a decent finish in recently—Pocono and Atlanta—were the ones with no bachelor events."

"That's coincidence," Gaby said, uneasy. "Besides, you won at Watkins Glen after a bachelor party."

"I always do well at the Glen."

She stepped out of his embrace. "Zack, the editor of *Now Woman* told me in confidence that, based on the votes they've received so far, you're neck and neck with Garrett Clark to win the contest."

His jaw dropped. "Really?"

"If you don't do the Richmond events, you're handing the bachelor title to Garrett. There's no way he won't show up, the guy's a publicity hog."

Unlike Zack, Garrett was also a shoo-in for the Chase.

"I have one last shot at making the Chase," Zack said. "I need to give it everything. If I make the Chase, Getaway won't give a damn about the bachelor contest."

"*If.*" Gaby let the loaded word sit between them, and tamped down the panic flaring inside her.

"I can do it."

"I believe you."

"Then let me pull out of the bachelor events."

Gaby gripped the edge of her desk. "That won't guarantee you'll make the Chase. There are seventeen drivers with enough points to have a shot at a top-twelve ranking. You can focus as much as you want, but it won't stop some guy crashing into you in his panic to get to the front."

"It's a risk," he agreed.

"If you miss out on both the Chase and the bachelor contest, Getaway will feel they have nowhere to go with this sponsorship." He stiffened, but she continued, "They'll pull their money, your season will be over. And with it, the ongoing relationship that being part of the team gives you with your family."

She tugged her blouse to straighten it where it had twisted during the kiss. "The bachelor contest is the safest bet. Getaway has a lot of faith in you—they're planning a huge ad campaign around you being Bachelor of the Year."

"Because they assume I won't make the Chase," he said, unimpressed. "Gaby, please, stand by me on this, ask Getaway to release me from the bachelor contest this weekend."

When he looked at her with that compelling combination of heat and hope in his eyes, she wanted more than anything to ease the tense lines around his mouth, take him in her arms, tell him she loved him. She'd do anything for him.

Gaby wondered if she could talk to Getaway, convince them Zack's best shot was to focus on the race, and that the bachelor events risked derailing him. Instead of sending him to the events at Richmond, Motor Media could maybe release a prerecorded interview with Zack this week, outside of the official events, but one that would get plenty of coverage and would convince women to vote for him in the contest….

"I don't know," she hedged, fretting.

Zack took her hands. "Gaby…I love you."

It took a second for the words to penetrate her anxiety. Her head snapped up. *"What?"*

"You heard me." He squeezed her fingers.

"You *love* me?"

"I—yeah. Seems that way." He sounded dazed.

She laughed, delight filtering through the tension, dissolving it. Zack's smile in response was gorgeously slow and sexy.

"So...do you love me, too?" he asked.

Something in his inflection, some air of expectancy, triggered a painful memory. If she answered yes, would Zack's next sentence start with *then?* As in, *Then you'll help me get out of the bachelor events at Richmond, right?*

Her chest constricted. Her fiancé had considered "I love you" to be a negotiating tool, and he'd said it with the same anticipatory tone.

"When did you realize you loved me?" she asked Zack, her voice a little sharp.

He pulled away. "Just now, I guess. I knew I cared for you, but I didn't realize how much."

"You've been mad at me, too mad to talk to me, and now you love me?"

"I apologized for that," he said, confused.

"And now that you want me to get you out of the bachelor events, you've decided you love me."

His eyes narrowed. "Don't be stupid," he said.

Oh, yeah, that was how a man spoke to the woman he loved, all right.

Gaby couldn't believe it. Once again, a man had asked her to risk her career, her ambitions, because he loved her. What was the bet that if she convinced Getaway to lighten up, and then Zack didn't make the Chase, that Gaby would miss out on her promotion? She could even lose her job, when it came out that she'd acted in Zack's interest rather than Getaway's.

She felt sick. And, to use Zack's word, stupid.

"What's stupid," she said, "is that you think I should risk my entire career because you don't want to attend a party and do an interview."

His face darkened. "Whereas you think I should risk *my* entire career just to go to that party and take part in that interview." He shoved his hands in his pockets. "I love you, dammit. And if you love me, you'll take my side in this."

Bingo.

If Zack really did love her, she'd be the happiest woman on the planet. Not feeling as if he was holding a prize just out of her reach, waiting for her to prove her worthiness.

"Then I don't love you," she lied.

Zack paled. She wanted to snatch the words back, she knew how keenly he felt rejection. But if his love wasn't genuine, and she knew it wasn't, even if he didn't, the pain would be short-lived.

"I guess we both know where we stand then," he said quietly.

See, he didn't even argue. Didn't try to convince her. He just left.

"TO RICHMOND." GRIMLY cheerful, Zack lifted his beer bottle in a toast.

Chad and Trent clinked their bottles against his. It was eleven o'clock on Tuesday night and they were alone at Matheson Racing. The race cars were ready to be hauled to Richmond tomorrow morning; the drivers and Chad would fly up in the afternoon.

"To the Chase," Trent said. More clinking.

It was all very well for Trent to toast the Chase, Zack thought. His younger brother had an excellent shot at making it, and he oozed the confidence of a man who intended to capitalize on his opportunities.

"To the Bachelor of the Year," Chad said, obviously wanting to offer something Zack had a good shot at. Zack decided to appreciate the gesture, rather than take it as an insult to his driving. Hell, he knew he'd only been invited to have a drink with the guys because Chad felt bad about Gaby and the whole family PR program thing.

Gaby. Her name made his gut ache. He'd told her he *loved* her, and she'd thrown it right back at him. Yeah, well, he was working at getting over the love thing. Hadn't he always sworn not to love a woman who couldn't put him first? Put their *relationship* first, he amended.

"You're quiet tonight, Zack." Chad grinned. "I mean, even quieter than usual. Worried about the race?"

"He has girl trouble," Trent speculated.

That was the annoying thing about Trent. Despite his self-centeredness, he was uncannily in tune with other people. Zack thought about denying it, given that both his brothers were blissfully married. But, hell, there was enough competition between them without getting caught up in that one. He lifted one shoulder. "Looks like Gaby and I are finished."

Chad eyed him closely. "Sorry to hear that."

"No, you're not," Zack said. "You were mad at her."

Chad laughed. He'd laughed so much since he and Brianna had gotten back together, sometimes he seemed like a different person. "Okay, I thought she was way out of line…you know, that day."

Zack realized from his brother's obscure words that Chad hadn't told Trent about the PR stunt Zack and Gaby had pulled on the family. The thought warmed him. He couldn't remember another occasion when he'd been privy to something Trent hadn't. Not since they were kids, when Zack and Chad had kept secrets from their annoying little brother.

"Thing is about Gaby—" Chad's voice saying her name startled Zack "—she's a real tiger about defending you."

Zack folded his arms. "Sometimes, yeah."

"Are you kidding? Don't you remember the way she laid into me and Dad?" Chad glanced at the curious Trent, obviously not wanting to elaborate.

She had laid into his father and Chad…but today, she'd refused to help him, and when she'd said she didn't love him, Zack had felt as if the sky had fallen down on him. He drained his beer, suddenly exhausted. "I'd better get going."

Chad eyed him critically. "Yeah, you need your beauty sleep if you're going to win that bachelor contest."

Zack forced a smile. No point mentioning he had no intention of attending the bachelor events. Richmond had to be all about the race.

"Time I left, too," Trent said, surprising Zack. Trent was a night owl, he seldom went to bed before midnight, and stayed up until two the night before a race.

They walked out to the near-empty parking lot. Trent had his hands in his pockets, his head down, unusually contemplative. Maybe he was nervous about the race, too.

When they reached Zack's truck, Zack drew a breath and said, "In case I don't get the chance to say it again—" or, more likely, in case he couldn't bring himself to say it again "—good luck making the Chase."

Trent's head jerked up in surprise, and Zack felt a twinge of shame.

"I'm sorry about you and Gaby," Trent said. "She's a great gal, and you deserve someone great."

Zack blinked—where did that come from? "These things happen," he said awkwardly.

"Not easy, though." Trent punched him sympathetically on the arm. "Gaby was good for you. Heck, you even seem like a nice guy when you're with her."

That was more the kind of taunt Zack was used to, but this time there was no sting with it. He smiled. He couldn't remember ever feeling so mellow toward his brother. "Gaby was good for me, but maybe not in the way you think." He found himself telling Trent about the "family PR campaign," about how calculated his good mood had been and how it had backfired.

"Man, I'd have loved to see Dad's face when he heard that one." Trent chuckled.

"Funnily enough, it's not one of my better memories." But Zack was smiling, too. "Anyway, I'm sorry I faked nice."

"Hey, you weren't *that* nice," Trent scoffed. Then he sobered. "You know, just because you were consciously working on the relationship, that doesn't mean you were faking it."

"How do you mean?"

Trent shrugged. "It's like me with my prerace routine. Just because Kelly spent a lot of time figuring out what worked and now that's what I do each week…yeah, it's contrived in that it's intentional, but it's still real. It's still me. It's just finding the part of me that works, and going with that, instead of all the other parts of me that get in the way of my racing."

"I hadn't thought of it like that," Zack said.

"I might not have done as well as you in school, but I'm not a total airhead."

Zack laughed, recalling that Trent and Kelly had met after she'd called him an airhead on national television. "Thanks, Trent," he said, his heart lighter than it had been since he'd fought with Gaby.

Which might have been a mistake, but he'd think about that after Richmond. This weekend, the race came first.

Zack opened the door of his truck.

"I have a confession to make, too," Trent said.

"What's that?"

Trent's gaze slid away. "That crash, four years ago…"

Zack froze. Around them, the night air turned suddenly chill, as if they'd been sucked into a refrigerator.

"Leave it, Trent." Zack didn't want to dwell on the past, not now.

Trent shook his head—he'd never taken orders from Zack before, why would he start now? "I always told you there was no way I could have avoided the crash," he said.

Zack heard the words in slo-mo, had a horrible feeling he knew exactly what was coming next. Every instinct screamed at him to stop his brother…and yet, it was like watching a car slide across the race track after it had hit the wall. Wanting to yell at the driver to *do something,* but knowing bigger forces were at work, that stopping it was beyond the realm of one man's powers.

"I lied," Trent said.

CHAPTER EIGHTEEN

THE WORDS HUNG THERE—stark, shocking, betrayal.

Zack took a step backward, bumped against his truck. "You knocked me out on purpose?"

The shake of Trent's head came as a relief. Because if Trent had crashed into him deliberately, the last eight months of effort had been pointless—there was no hope they could ever be part of the same family.

"But I didn't go out of my way to avoid you," Trent confessed.

Zack's mouth dried; his words came out chalky. "Meaning what?"

"I could have steered around you." Trent swallowed. "There was time." No one was a better judge than Trent of the finer nuances of an opportunity to pass. "But there was a chance—a good chance—I'd have scraped Justin Murphy."

"Scraped." Zack tried to make sense of it.

"Scraped, nudged, bumped." The wave of Trent's hand indicated impatience with semantics. "Probably not a big scrape. I was pretty sure I could get away with it…but not a hundred percent."

"You didn't want to risk Murphy retaliating," Zack said.

"You know what he's like when something gets his dander up." The old-fashioned word was one of Brady's favorites— the thought of his father and the rift between them, which had been made worse by the events of the day they were talking about, made Zack's chest ache. Trent said, "I didn't want Murphy coming after me and putting me out of the race."

Four years ago, that might well have happened, Zack conceded. Justin Murphy was a more mature, settled driver now, and so was Trent. But back then, they'd all had something to prove.

"So you had a choice," he said. "Scrape Murphy, then spend the rest of the race watching your back, or put me into the wall and get clear ahead."

Trent looked as if he wanted to deny that the choice had been that bald, that selfish. But he said, "Yeah."

"And you knew that putting me into the wall would likely mean I couldn't make the Chase." *Because let's be quite clear about the consequences of that decision.* Zack almost hoped his brother would deny it...though Trent was plenty smart enough to have figured it all out.

"Yeah," Trent said.

Zack felt as if someone had his heart in their fist and was twisting, squeezing. Back then, bitterly disappointed, he'd accused Trent of deliberately sacrificing him. Deep down, he hadn't believed it. Hadn't believed his own brother could do that.

Now...he didn't know what to think. A mishmash of emotions pummeled him. Anger, betrayal, relief that the past four years of strain hadn't been entirely his fault.

"Why are you telling me this now?" he demanded. "Are you trying to mess with my head, psych me out for Richmond?"

"No!" Trent recoiled. "I wanted to tell you you're a great driver. That you have every chance of making the Chase—that getting knocked out four years ago wasn't your fault. I don't want that hanging over you." He tipped his head back, so he was gazing at the sky. "I was so relieved when you said you were coming back, I thought we could put the past behind us. But it's not that simple, is it?"

Zack shook his head.

"That's why I told you. I hope, when you get over the shock, it'll help."

Was Trent crazy? How could it help to know his own brother had betrayed him?

"Zack." Trent's voice deepened. "I'm sorry." He opened his mouth as if to say more, then he shut up.

Zack appreciated that. No excuses, no explanations.

Trent turned and walked away toward his fancy sports car.

Zack sank into the driver's seat of the truck, his mind reeling. Trent had hit him, pretty much deliberately…Zack's anger hadn't been unjustified…the choice had come down to him or Trent, and Trent had—

It was too much to handle right now. Maybe he could go see Gaby.

No. Zack hunched his shoulders. Gaby had made it clear where she stood, and it was no longer with him.

"WHAT DO YOU MEAN, you can't find Zack?" Sandra looked so mad, Gaby wondered if it was possible to induce early labor by gnashing your teeth.

Gaby glanced out the window of the Matheson Racing hospitality suite. *He's somewhere out there.* Her stomach roiled. Despite everything, she'd clung to the hope that Zack would turn up to this morning's sponsor briefing, then to the bachelor events scheduled for tonight and tomorrow morning. That he'd meant what he said about loving her, and he would want to be here for her.

Nuh-uh. It was just Gaby, Sandra and two very unhappy clients.

"I guess he had something important to do for the race." Gaby at least wanted to remind them there was a bigger picture here.

"I want to give him this for tonight." Rob Hudson held up a dress shirt with the Getaway Resorts logo on it. "We had it made specially."

She had to give them the bad news. "I'm afraid Zack feels his racing—and your sponsorship—is best served by him focusing on the race. He won't be at the bachelor party and there won't be any Olivia Winton interview." She'd called Winton's staff to cancel.

Rob Hudson slammed his hand down on the table. "We're paying him to attend those events. He doesn't get to pull out whenever the fancy takes him, not if he wants to keep our money."

"This is totally unacceptable—you need to find your client," Sandra told her, distancing herself from Gaby— normally it was *our* client. She folded her arms over her stomach. "If you want that promotion, Gaby, you will find Zack, and you will get him to the party and the Olivia Winton interview, and he'll be on his best behavior."

"Tell him if he doesn't show up, he won't have a sponsor," Hudson said.

He didn't sound as if he was bluffing. Images flitted through Gaby's head. Her promotion, gone. Maybe even her job. And with it, her hope for independence.

She nodded wordlessly, gathered her papers and headed outside.

She had to find Zack. When she did, she would tear a strip off him and if necessary, drug him and drag him to that interview tomorrow.

She headed for the motor home park, but the guard wouldn't let her in without Zack's authorization. She called his cell; no answer. She tried Trent, and luckily he was in his motor home. He came out to escort Gaby into the lot.

"I need to find Zack," she said. "He didn't show up at the sponsor briefing—I need to convince him to come to the bachelor events."

Was it her imagination, or did Trent look shifty?

"Getaway said they'll pull out if he doesn't turn up." It was risky, telling Trent that, but she was desperate.

Trent swore. "He was in his motor home earlier. Maybe he's just not answering his phone."

At Zack's motor home, Gaby knocked on the door.

"Do it like this," Trent said. He pounded on the door with his fist and yelled, "Zack, you chicken-livered son of a gun, open up!"

Gaby took a step back in alarm.

Zack didn't answer the door.

"That brother of mine needs to face facts," Trent said, minus his usual lighthearted demeanor.

"What's going on?" Gaby asked.

"Ah, hell, I guess I have to tell you, too," Trent said, disgusted. "Come back to my place."

"I don't have time, I have to find Zack."

"There's something you need to know," Trent said.

In Trent's state-of-the-art motor home, Gaby sat on a leather couch, Kelly curled up beside her. Trent took a seat on the other side of the living area. He leaned forward, hands clasped between his knees. "I'll tell you exactly what I told Zack last night."

By the time he finished, Gaby was trembling with shock and anger. "All these years," she accused, "you let him carry the responsibility for the breakdown of your relationship."

"I'm sorry," Trent said.

Kelly patted Gaby's hand sympathetically; she'd obviously heard this before. Or maybe, being a psychologist, she was unshockable.

"I know Zack's a jerk sometimes," Trent concluded. *Runs in the family,* Gaby thought, eyeing his handsome face. "But maybe he has a good reason."

It couldn't have been easy for Trent to confess to Zack, she realized.

"What are you going to do?" Kelly asked her. "There's a lot at stake."

She meant more than Zack's sponsorship, Gaby knew. And in that moment, Gaby realized there was more than her promotion at stake, too. She loved Zack—nothing he said or did could change that.

She thought about Sandra's and Getaway's threats. If Zack's declaration of love had been an attempt to manipulate her, what had Sandra and Getaway been doing, if not manipulation of their own?

There was no escaping that other people would try and use her for their own purposes and benefit. She had to decide whether or not to let them.

"If anyone's going to manipulate me," she said, "I want it to be Zack."

Trent looked charmingly confused, but Kelly nodded.

"He likes to insist he's single-minded about his racing," Gaby continued, "but if you knew how much time he spends thinking about you guys, and Brady, and Chad..."

"Family matters to him," Trent admitted. "No doubt about it."

"He's misguided," she said, mainly to herself. "And he screws up—heck, does he ever screw up. But at heart, he's a tender, loving guy."

"Okay, that's enough," Trent said. Kelly threw a balled-up piece of paper at him but he dodged it.

Gaby stood. She headed for the door of the motor home.

"Where are you going?" Trent asked.

"Zack's heart needs protecting," she said, "and I'm the woman for the job."

THE GARAGE AT RICHMOND was the usual hive of activity the day before the race, so Zack figured it was just him who felt as if everything was happening on mute, at a distance. It was as if he was in a vacuum—standing outside the hauler all alone, while around him, people went about their business. He hadn't seen Gaby since she'd rejected his declaration of love, he wasn't calm enough to talk to Trent, and Chad and Brady were occupied with their own concerns.

If Zack made the Chase, it would be all on his own efforts. At least he wasn't doing those damn bachelor events. He should feel relieved. More confident about the race. But he

didn't. He ached all over. Not the physical ache from racing
that grew more pronounced the older you got—this ache was
an awareness of a whole lot of things missing from his life.
A knowledge that he'd screwed up.

Most of all, it was an I-miss-Gaby ache.

He tipped his head back, let the sun fall on his face.
Sounds penetrated the cocoon he'd built around himself.
Dave calling to the jackman. The hiss of an air gun as a
tire was inflated. Two mechanics conferring loudly near the
No. 548 car.

Beyond the garage, the buzz of fans had grown steadily in
the last hour. On the infield, RVs maneuvered into position,
the yells of frustrated dads mingling with the shrieks of over-
excited kids.

Behind him, two fans high-fived each other as they
snagged Kent Grosso's autograph.

Zack absorbed it all—the sights, the sounds, the smells—
and let the spirit of the race track seep into him. He looked
around for someone who was as alone as he was…and didn't
find anyone. The fans, the teams, everyone was part of a
group that gave them a sense of identity. Each group had a
goal for the weekend, whether it was enjoying the race
together, or teaming up to produce a winning race car.

In a blaze of clarity, the truth hit Zack. No way had he
gotten here all on his own efforts. NASCAR wasn't a
solitary sport—it couldn't be. Winning races was about
being a team.

He might not be seeing eye to eye with many people right
now, but his team was building the No. 548 car for the race
at Richmond with all the dedication as if he was a hot contender for the Chase. They deserved victory—and if Zack
didn't make it, it wouldn't be their fault.

It would be Zack's. Because he'd cut himself off. From his
family, who loved him in their screwed-up way. Today, from
the fans who would not only vote for him in the bachelor

contest, but who also gave him encouragement that any driver needed out on the track. From Gaby, the woman he loved.

He'd asked her to take an enormous leap of faith—to risk her promotion, her future, for his decidedly shaky racing— and offered her nothing in return. Sure, he'd muttered something about love, as surprised to hear himself say it as she was. But beyond that…

His poor sweetheart. He groaned, drawing attention from a passing mechanic. Zack gave the guy a thumbs-up. He knew how wary Gaby was, how scared she was that a man would use her only to leave her again. He'd done nothing to reassure her. How could he demand that she prove her love for him, when he wasn't willing to do the same?

I'm a jerk. Zack ran a hand through his hair and faced the facts.

He could afford to lose the race. He couldn't afford to lose Gaby.

RYAN SPENT MOST OF the NASCAR Nationwide Series race at Richmond fuming about Amber's unreasonable attitude, the way she'd decided he was a sleaze when *she* was the one who'd said she didn't want a serious relationship.

After that disastrous last date, he'd talked to his father and grandfather about Billy Blake, so he had some idea of where she was coming from. But it wasn't as if he'd tried to deceive her or pretend he was anything he wasn't.

Next time he saw her, he thought as he passed last year's NASCAR Nationwide Series champion, he wasn't going to let her get away with all that yelling. Nope, if anyone around here had a right to yell, it was him. She was out of line.

He wished she was here. He floored it past two more cars, almost pinging the wall.

Amber had been right about one thing. Ryan did love to race, but recently he'd been racing for his dad and granddad, for the Thorne tradition. It hadn't been about his passion, as it should be. And when he really thought about what he might say when he saw her again, he didn't want to yell at her at all. He wanted, of all things, to look after her.

How soon could he get out of this car and tell her so?

"How many laps to go, Dad?" he said into his headset.

His dad made a choking sound. Then, in what had to be the most surreal moment of his life, Ryan saw the checkered flag ahead. Huh? How did that come up so fast? Who had passed it already?

No one, he realized, as he sped over the line to claim his first ever win in the series.

In Victory Lane, he hauled himself out of his car, hugged his father and grandfather, winced under Brady's hearty slap on the back, gave the obligatory interviews and smiles for the cameras. Everything passed in such a blur that he couldn't take it all in. Finally, they headed for the motor home.

"That was better than the race I won at Nashville," his grandfather said, a gleam of reminiscence in his eyes.

"This is it, son," his father said. "You're on your way."

Ryan felt oddly lighthearted. "I'm on my way," he agreed. "I'm on *my* way," he amended, knowing the change of emphasis was lost on his seniors.

He wasn't going anywhere without Amber.

"Dad, Grandpa, I know you guys are excited and you want to celebrate," he said, "but can I meet you back in the motor home in a half hour? There's something I need to do."

He left the older men and headed for Brady's motor home. He wasn't sure Amber would have watched the race, but when she opened the door to him, she said a cool, "Congratulations."

"You need to come with me," he said, so seriously that she blanched.

"Why? Is something wrong?"

"Kind of, it concerns your mom," Ryan said. Because there *was* something wrong with Julie-Anne—she had a crappy relationship with her daughter. Besides, he wasn't sure he'd get Amber out the door if he told her what he really wanted.

When they arrived at his parents' motor home, she balked. "What's this about?"

"There's someone waiting to talk to you in here. About your mom...and other things."

The look she gave him was deeply suspicious, but she followed him inside.

She'd met his mother before; the two women exchanged greetings. Then Ryan introduced Amber to his dad, Jeff, and grandfather.

"Dad, Grandad," Ryan said, "I want you to tell Amber about her father."

Amber stiffened. "What is this?"

Ryan grabbed her hand. "Before you go accusing me, or anyone else, of being like Billy Blake, I want you to know how he fit in around here, what other people thought of him."

Amber tried to pull away, but he held on to her. "Please, Amber," he said. "Do it for us."

Her eyes widened, but she said, "You still trying to get me into bed?"

He might have known she wouldn't hold back just because his family was there. His mom gave a shocked gasp. Ryan felt himself color, but he held her gaze. "I'm trying to get you into my life."

Heck, that wasn't a fraction of what he needed to say to her, but the rest was private. He just needed to keep her here long enough so he got the chance to say it.

Some of the tension left her fingers. She gave a jerky nod. Ryan steered her to the couch and sat next to her. He still held her hand, in case she got any ideas about running away again.

"Billy Blake," his grandfather said, "was the meanest man I ever met."

Amber started, but Granddad continued, "You might not want to hear this, little lady, but I tell it like I see it."

"That's fine," she said.

"He had a way with the ladies," Granddad said. "He made the most of it."

"He wasn't a bad driver," Jeff said.

"When he didn't have a hangover or a grudge," Granddad conceded. "But there's a hell of a lot more to making it as a NASCAR driver than how well you put the car around the oval. Attitude," he said sagely. "And Billy Blake was one big bundle of bad attitude."

CHAPTER NINETEEN

AMBER KNEW THAT. BUT hearing it from someone on the inside of the sport was a new experience.

"You know your dad got fired shortly before the accident?" Jeff asked.

Amber nodded.

"We drivers were surprised it had taken so long. We all knew Billy Blake would never make it in NASCAR. It was just a matter of how soon his flashy veneer would fall apart in front of the wrong person."

"When you heard him kissing up to a team owner you had to smile," Ryan's grandpa said. "It was a polished performance, all right."

"My mom…" she began, not sure what she wanted to say.

"Your mother was the main reason anyone spoke to Billy at all," Granddad said. "She was a brave little thing. She had to know Billy was cheating on her—he didn't bother to hide his flings from anyone except his boss—but she'd show up every weekend, you in tow."

"A good woman, that Julie-Anne," Jeff agreed. "Always a kind word, always ready to help out."

"She did everything she could to help your dad," Grandpa said. "And the rest of us did what we could. But some folk are beyond helping."

"Someone helped him by bringing him whisky," Amber said.

"So-called friends," Jeff said dismissively. "Your daddy had a bunch of hangers-on who were never going to get any closer to anyone famous. Giving him booze was their passport to his fame." He shook his head. "I tried talking sense to one of them myself once, told him to cut it out. He couldn't see what the problem was."

"After the accident—" Amber's voice sounded rusty "—Mom sent me away. She stayed with him."

She couldn't believe she'd said that, to a room full of near strangers. Then Ryan laced his fingers through hers. For a guy who wanted nothing more than a casual fling, he sure was making an effort. Amber squeezed back and felt the simultaneous clenching of her stomach muscles.

"Just about killed her, that did," Granddad said.

Amber stared. "What makes you say that?"

"She had this edge to her," Jeff said. "Like she was on the brink. No one expected her to stick with Billy very long. But then he had the accident. Then he got the cancer. Damn shame, if you ask me, that he lasted longer than the few months the doctors said."

He leaned back against the wall. "Julie-Anne was heart-broken." He nodded to Amber. "We all knew it was about you being gone, not about your dad's illness." He sighed. "That's it, really. The whole thing was a damn shame."

It was more than that, Amber wanted to say. *It was the end of my childhood.* Yet how much worse must it have been for her mom? Tears threatened.

"When I think about what NASCAR means to our family," Jeff said, "I would say your mom felt like that about our sport, but your dad didn't. Doesn't make much sense, I know, given he was the driver. But for him, racing NASCAR was a means to an end. Fame and fortune."

"Whereas for us, it's about passion," Granddad said.

Amber could see that. These men were like Brady, like her stepbrothers.

"Dad, Grandad," Ryan said, "you've been great." The dismissal in his voice was unmistakable.

"He wins one race and he thinks he can order us around," his father joked. But he stood up anyway.

"Actually," Ryan said, "I wasn't asking you to leave, just changing the subject."

His father sat down again.

"What you just said, about what NASCAR means to our family," Ryan began. "I couldn't have put it better."

"Thanks, son."

"I realized recently that I've lost sight of that," Ryan said. "When I first started in NASCAR, every race was a high. The days in between races were truly frustrating."

His grandfather chuckled.

"But I lost that," Ryan said. "Somewhere along the way, I let go of my dream and started living yours, and I haven't enjoyed myself since."

It was as if he'd switched to Swahili—the two faces opposite him blanked. Amber held her breath.

"I want to race NASCAR, make no mistake," Ryan reassured his dad and grandfather. "But I need to do it for me. I'll always need your support, I'll always get a kick out of your racing stories—the first time I hear them, at least." He grinned, removing the sting. "But what I want is to race for me."

Amber stared. Had Ryan come to these conclusions because of what she'd said? Had he taken the words she'd uttered in anger, and considered the underlying truth? Every time she thought he was a shallow jerk, he displayed a level of insight that floored her.

His father removed his spectacles, began to polish them. He said slowly, "You have to be your own man, Ryan. I wouldn't want it any other way."

It was a big concession, Amber knew. One that showed Jeff truly loved his son.

It seemed Ryan was intent on pushing that love to its limits. He drew a breath and said, "Thanks, Dad, I appreciate that.

But I have to tell you, it seems…it seems there's something I want more than I want to race NASCAR."

Identical expressions of dismay stole over his father's and grandfather's faces, replacing their cautious relief.

Ryan took Amber's hands in his, looked deep into her eyes. *Me? He wants me?* Her heart leapt.

"If Amber doesn't want me to race NASCAR—if, because of her father, she has difficulties with that," Ryan said, scarcely glancing at his audience, "then I'll figure out something else to do."

Ryan would give up his NASCAR dream? She shook her head; he nodded, his mouth widening into the cocky grin she loved. Loved? Oh, yes, she was falling for this man like it was going out of fashion.

He hadn't said he loved her—he probably thought she'd say it was too soon. But he'd made more of a commitment to her in that one sentence than anyone else had, ever.

Except, maybe, her mom. In her heart, Amber knew Julie-Anne had never stopped loving her, missing her. That she'd been in a situation where doing the right thing was torture, and so would have been doing the wrong thing.

She noticed Ryan's parents and grandfather were slipping out the door. The silence that fell was heavy with anticipation.

"You meant that," Amber said, "about giving up racing."

Ryan sighed. "Yep. I know it's crazy—you're the biggest pain in the butt I ever failed to date."

She laughed.

"But I need you," he said. "With you around, stuff matters."

"Stuff?"

"It's hard to explain," he said, endearingly sheepish. "Can you just accept that I know what I want, and it starts and ends with you?"

"Yeah, I guess I can." Amber leaned forward and kissed him. She meant it to be just a swift kiss, but it turned into something sweet and tender, then hotly passionate.

His hands roamed over her, seeking a familiarity, an intimacy, that would bind them. *Yes,* Amber thought. She'd never felt like this before.

"So," she gasped, "we're alone, you must have a bed…"

"No way," Ryan said.

She pulled back, met his rueful gaze. *"No?"*

"If I make love to you now, you'll figure out some way to turn it into me being a jerk who only ever wanted a roll in the hay."

"I won't." She thought about it, about the insecurities that might have been dealt a mortal blow today, but which weren't dead yet. "I guess I might."

He squeezed her behind. "A risk I'm not prepared to take, sweetheart. We won't make love until you're certain this is forever. Which I suspect will probably require a walk down the aisle."

Her heart swelled and she wanted to laugh. Instead, she forced a scowl. "You're so young," she said cuttingly.

He laughed for her. "You're so mine." He kissed her again.

"If we don't get to make love," she grumbled, "I suppose I might as well go talk to my mom."

He kissed her again. "Shall I come with you?"

How she loved him for offering! "Thanks, but there'll probably be crying."

He shuddered. "I would come, you know."

"I know." She kissed him, reveling in the tender emotion, the openness of his feelings for her. "But I need to do this on my own. Then I'll be all yours."

GABY COULD BARELY KEEP her eyes open, despite the noise and the stimulation of being in the pits at Richmond on race day. She'd spent Friday afternoon, most of Friday night, then all day today crunching the numbers on Zack's sponsorship. On every measure, she'd proven that Getaway Resorts got its money's worth—*more* than its money's worth—from Zack.

Was it enough to convince Getaway they hadn't suffered

from Zack's ducking out of the bachelor events? Enough to keep Zack's sponsorship intact so he could finish the season that was so important to him? And maybe, just maybe, keep her own job?

Gaby blinked against a haze of exhaustion as she passed Trent's pits. Trent had qualified fifth. She could see Zack's pits, and the electric blue war wagon, up ahead.

Uh-oh, there was Sandra. Gaby slowed, despite the fact she was looking for her boss. She hadn't talked to Sandra since that meeting yesterday morning. She'd ignored Sandra's calls. Gaby didn't know of anyone who'd done that and lived to tell the tale. She swallowed, wiped her hands against her caramel-colored pants, then clutched her satchel closer.

Two Getaway guys stood next to Sandra, increasing Gaby's trepidation. And next to them, Chad. Who knew how he felt about her at the moment?

One way to find out. Gaby found pinning on a smile wasn't as difficult as she'd thought it would be. She'd done the right thing, and she had good news. They just had to listen.

Chad saw her first, and a big smile broke out, the kind he normally only wore for Brianna. "Gaby, we were just talking about you."

"Hi, Gaby." Sandra sounded thoughtful rather than vengeful.

"I'm glad I found you all here." Sandra didn't look as if she was about to fire her, but that could be her "company" face. For Zack's sake, Gaby needed to make her point fast. She flipped open her satchel and pulled out her presentation folder. "I've been looking into the return on investment Getaway gets from the money it spends on Zack," she began. "You need to see this."

Over the next ten minutes, awkwardly juggling the folder as she flipped pages and pointed at vital facts, she explained the weighting she'd given to different media impressions, the equation she'd used to attach a value to those impressions, the calculations she'd made. She employed every persuasive power at her disposal, fielded questions with aplomb. All the time, she was aware of Sandra's silence, and Rob Hudson's poker face.

At last, she concluded, "Whatever Zack does out on the track—win, lose or crash—you get a return that would be the envy of many marketers. When he wins, you maximize that investment fivefold. Letting Zack focus on his racing at the expense of the bachelor contest costs you nothing, and potentially increases your return to astronomic levels—even if he doesn't make the Chase."

She stopped, and the cumulative effect of sleep deprivation and emotional stress caught up with her. She almost swayed, locked her knees to stay upright. Then she realized Sandra was clapping.

"Excllent work, Gaby," her boss said warmly. "I've never seen such a thorough analysis—and I thought I was a numbers freak." Everyone else laughed; the best Gaby could muster was a dazed smile.

"Very interesting," Rob Hudson admitted. "I'm not going to rush into agreeing with you, but you've certainly given us a lot to think about."

It wasn't a wholesale endorsement, but it was progress.

"Come on, Rob," Sandra said with the brusque assertiveness her clients loved. "This stuff is pure gold."

He laughed. "I'm considering it, Sandra."

"I should think so," Sandra scolded. "Gaby's work is phenomenal."

Gaby felt strangely light-headed, to the point where she didn't care either way what they thought of her work. She'd done her best for Zack. The rest was up to him.

"Where is he?" she asked Chad.

He knew who she meant. "Over the wall—they're just about to start the national anthem." Gaby became aware of a brass band playing in the background. Chad put an arm around her shoulder, a very un-Chad-like gesture. "I was just telling Sandra how Zack's had a busy couple of days with the bachelor contest events."

Gaby froze. "What?"

Chad chuckled. "Zack went to the bachelor party last night, then had an interview with Olivia Winton this morning."

"But I canceled—"

"And I reinstated the interview, at Zack's request."

Gaby's mind raced. Why had Zack gone to the contest events, when he'd been so adamant he wouldn't?

There was only one possible explanation. He'd done it for her. Because it was important to her. Of course, by then she'd already been acting on the conclusion she'd reached with Trent and Kelly, that she was sick of her boss manipulating her, but he wouldn't have known that.

Zack cared about her, more than she'd dreamed.

She wanted to leap over the pit wall and stick her head in the window of the No. 548 car, tell Zack she loved him. But even as she took a step in that direction, the grand marshal announced, "Gentlemen, start your engines."

Later, she told herself as the cars circled the track, getting ready to race. She just had to hope that the outcome of the race—she had awful visions of Zack crashing early and destroying his hopes of making the Chase—wouldn't change the way he felt.

Across the track, the green flag fell, and the air filled with the roar of forty-three cars, every single one of them hungry for victory. *Time to pray.*

CHAPTER TWENTY

FROM ABOUT LAP TEN, Zack struggled to keep his focus. The start of the evening race had, as always, demanded full concentration, but now that he'd passed Kent Grosso—*good*—and been passed by Danny Cruise—*bad*—and settled into a groove that kept him in the same twelfth place he'd qualified in, his mind began to wander.

To Gaby, of course. He wished he'd seen her before the race. He couldn't shake the feeling that if he'd been able to kiss her, to convey how he felt, it would have been better for his racing. Too late now, he couldn't let that kind of superstition affect him. He had to finish in the top ten to secure his place in the Chase regardless of what any other driver did. If a couple of the drivers already in the top twelve crashed out, he might be able to get away with a slightly lower finish.

Putting Gaby out of his mind only opened it to thoughts of his family. Zack had asked Chad to fix up the Olivia Winton interview, and to come to the bachelor party with him. His brother had joined him, no questions asked, providing welcome moral support among the sea of women. Olivia Winton had been there, filming a presegment for this morning's show, and some of the things Chad had said to her about Zack, which Olivia had relayed to him during his interview this morning…. Chad wasn't prone to exaggeration, so Zack knew he must have meant them. His brother's words were so flattering that Zack was pretty sure he'd blushed on national television.

Zack grinned at the memory. Maybe one day he'd have Chad on about that. For now, he was enjoying the glow of having a big brother who rated him so highly.

Zack saw Trent's No. 429 car up ahead. His stomach knotted, destroying the momentary peace of mind. The tension gave him a burst of speed and he passed Will Branch. If he could do that a few more times, he might have a shot of making the Chase. He thought some more about Trent, since that seemed to be what had given him the impetus to make the pass.

Trent and his confession about that ill-fated race. When Zack thought about the animosity he'd felt over the past few years—the loneliness—he wanted to punch his brother. Almost without noticing, he passed Justin Murphy. Murphy held up two fingers, the wrong way to mean peace. Zack grinned and held on to his hostility through yet another pass. He was in the lead pack now, somewhere in the top ten, he figured.

It was a good place to be, and Zack held on to it through several pit stops. He wondered if Gaby was out there in the shadows, watching his progress around the track, which was lit up brighter than day. Or if she'd given up on him.

Then it was the final pit stop. Zack needed all four tires changed and a decent amount of gas put in his car, which meant he was in the pits a couple of seconds longer than some of his rivals. Two seconds could make all the difference. He fought to retain his self-control as he headed back out along pit road. If he did something stupid now, he'd earn a penalty and totally blow it.

He made it back onto the track without mishap, and was pretty sure he heard a sigh of relief over his headphones.

He passed Trey Sanford, which put him right behind Trent. "Gap," his spotter said a lap later. His chance to pass his brother. On the backstretch, he moved up alongside Trent. Neck and neck. Zack looked straight ahead.

"Trouble low," Zack's spotter said, with sudden urgency in his voice. Zack could see it now, smoke and a cloud of dust—Danny Cruise's car sat on the infield. Danny had already qualified for the Chase, so Zack didn't waste time feeling sorry for him. On the track, near the pole line, there was still a tangle of two or three cars, at least one of them a lapped car. Zack held his line, even though it meant getting dangerously close to the melee.

"Zack," Chad cautioned through the headphones. Huh, Chad was still with him? Zack had assumed he'd be on Trent's channel right now.

Dammit, Zack couldn't sit alongside Trent any longer. He had to get ahead. Once they were no longer under caution, Zack quickly looked for a gap and he saw one coming into Turn Three, even before his spotter pointed it out. They were coming up to a lapped car—they'd have to go three-wide for a second or two, but that wasn't a problem at Richmond. As he got closer, he realized he'd overestimated the size of the gap. There probably wasn't a driver on the track who could make it through there without tangling with the lapped rookie. Or without pushing Trent into the wall.

Zack's heart beat faster. It wouldn't actually be *pushing* Trent into the wall. More a little nudge that would leave his brother nowhere to go. Zack would simply be doing what he had to in order to get ahead. Easier, safer than messing with the rookie. With the unexpected bonus of payback against his brother.

Do it, he told himself. He glanced across at Trent. There had to be a couple of feet of space between them, but right now, it felt like nothing. Trent looked back at him, and Zack imagined he could see behind his brother's visor. See resignation in Trent's eyes, and acceptance that this was his due.

Sorry, kid.

How long was it since Zack had thought of Trent as his kid brother? These days, it was always Trent up ahead.

Zack thought about the imminent smash, what it would do to the family. No matter that Trent deserved it, they'd be back where they were at the start of this season. Bitterest rivals, rather than brothers. Who knew how long it would take to recover this time?

But, dammit, Zack needed to make the Chase, even more than Trent did.

Back off, he told Trent telepathically. *Let me pass and I won't have to put you into the wall.*

Because if he hit Trent, no matter if Zack won this race, made the Chase, won the whole series, he'd have lost the battle he'd been fighting since January. The battle for his family, for a true team.

He couldn't do it; the certainty settled in, wouldn't be shaken. Trent hadn't eased off at the prospect of hitting the wall—he would always give it everything, no matter what the risk. Damn. Zack had to make a clean pass.

Anyone watching the race would say it was impossible for Zack to make the pass before they reached the corner where Trent would be pushed into the wall.

Zack dug within himself, mined every reserve of strength, of speed, of strategy, of adrenaline. Hit the floor with the gas pedal. Slowly, he pulled ahead of Trent. The gap was minuscule now, the corner almost upon them. Impossible. Still, Zack kept going.

He squeaked through by the narrowest of margins, practically brushing panels with Trent. But not actually touching him. Nor did he touch the rookie.

Zack whooped as he surged ahead, and got an answering whoop in his ear from Chad. The crowd surged to its feet, cheering. *For me.* Zack found himself grinning like an idiot. Three more laps to go, a couple of easy passes, then he blistered past the checkered flag behind Bart Branch and someone else.

"Third," Chad yelled into the headset. "You did it, bro, you made the Chase. You're the man."

"Yeah, yeah." Zack fought the speed wobble as the car slowed down. He laughed out loud.

He was in the Chase. But he wasn't done yet.

GABY HAD SCREAMED SO much during the race, she was just about hoarse. She raced to the pit wall, past Julie-Anne and Amber, who were hugging each other and crying, and past Ryan Thorne, who was doing a good job of crashing their embrace. Past Chad and Brianna, who were celebrating Zack's result with a kiss that positively smoked. Past Brady, beaming from ear to ear as he divided his attention between his family here in the pits, and his sons out on the track.

"Gaby, wait up," Sandra called.

Gaby ignored her. Her knees pressed against the wall as she scanned the pit road for Zack's car. She'd been so scared for him—for *them*—when she'd realized he intended to attempt that pass....

Here he came now.

"I've…been thinking," Sandra wheezed next to her, breathless from her brisk waddle. "About the promotion."

"Uh-huh." Gaby strained to see Zack's face. She thought she caught a glimpse of his grin. She couldn't wait to kiss him. She caught the occasional word from Sandra—*exceptional performance…difficult driver…someone I can trust…capable hands*—but she wasn't really listening.

Zack clambered out the window of the No. 548 car and pulled off his helmet. His smile was filled with elation…and when he saw Gaby, he positively glowed. Gaby caught her breath.

"Have you heard a word I said?" Sandra sounded half-annoyed, half-amused.

"Uh, no, sorry, Sandra." Gaby didn't take her eyes off Zack.

Sandra pffed. "Ah, well, there's always later. But don't leave it too long—I seem to have swelled up like a balloon today. I think my doctor's going to have me on bedrest any day now."

That did distract Gaby. She looked at her boss in alarm. "Are you all right?"

She rolled her eyes. "*Now* she's interested. Get back to your sweetheart, Gaby." When Gaby gaped, Sandra said, "Yes, I know how you feel about Zack, it's been obvious for weeks. I thought I'd give you a chance to prove you could handle it…and you did great." She put a finger under Gaby's chin and gently closed her mouth. "I'll call you from home tomorrow. If Gideon will let me."

"Gaby," Zack said.

Gaby turned around, just in time for Zack to haul her into his arms for a crushing hug. He smelled of sweat and oil. He smelled like her dreams.

She wrapped her arms around him. He lowered his mouth to hers. But before he could kiss her, he said, "I'm a jerk."

"I know," she said happily.

One strong hand cupped her behind. "I love you."

"I know," she said on a dreamy sigh. Had there ever been a moment better than this?

He laughed. "I'm sorry I was so selfish—and if you say you know—"

"Kiss me," she said. "I love you, too."

Now he did kiss her, with a fire and an energy that shouldn't have been possible after the grueling race he'd just endured. But Zack was good at the impossible.

"From now on, we're a team," he said. "We'll make it work so that we both get what we want."

"I want *you*," she said.

He grinned. "And I want you. More than anything. So maybe this doesn't have to be too hard."

He pushed a strand of hair behind her ear, infinitely gentle. "I'm so proud of you."

She blinked. "You just stole my line."

"Uh-uh." He kissed the tip of her nose. "I love the way you fight for what's right. You're the best PR rep NASCAR has ever seen. I'd better marry you before some other driver figures that out."

Her heart swelled. "You're the best man I know."

"And the best damned Matheson," Trent said. He'd finished seventh, also making the Chase, and had rushed straight to see his brother. "You did a good thing," he told Zack. "A big thing."

"Yeah, well, it won't happen again." Zack relinquished Gaby just long enough to give his brother an awkward hug, then he pulled her back into his arms.

"Where was I?" he asked.

"Proposing?" she suggested hopefully.

"Wow, you really do know everything." He kissed her.

A shriek came from Sandra, drawing everyone's attention. Taney, who was crossing the pits, sprinted the last few steps to his wife. "Sweetheart? Is it the baby?"

"Of course not." Sandra winked at Gaby as she held up her cell phone. "I just got a call from the editor of *Now Woman*. They're about to announce the official results of the bachelor contest. Zack, you need to get over to the contest suite."

His jaw dropped. "You mean—"

Sandra laughed. "Yep, for some reason, the women of America chose the grumpiest man in NASCAR as bachelor of the year."

Chad and Trent started a round of catcalls and hollering that would make anyone think they were teenage goofballs.

Brady scratched his head. "Well, I'll be."

"Makes perfect sense to me." Gaby kissed Zack, and he kissed her right back. "After all, you *are* a hottie."

Zack laughed. "I have to warn you all," he announced to his family, to Sandra, to anyone who would listen. "I'm not sure how long I'll hold the Bachelor of the Year title. If Gaby will have me, I won't be a bachelor much longer."

Laughter and cheering rippled around. Zack gazed down at Gaby, his eyes filled with love. "Will you marry me, Gaby? Be my wife, my partner, my better half?"

"Just try and stop me." Gaby tugged him close, and lost herself in Zack Matheson's kiss.

* * * * *

REQUEST YOUR FREE BOOKS!

2 FREE NOVELS
FROM THE ROMANCE COLLECTION
PLUS 2 FREE GIFTS!

YES! Please send me 2 FREE novels from the Romance Collection and my 2 FREE gifts (gifts are worth about $10). After receiving them, if I don't wish to receive any more books, I can return the shipping statement marked "cancel." If I don't cancel, I will receive 4 brand-new novels every month and be billed just $5.74 per book in the U.S. or $6.24 per book in Canada. That's a saving of at least 28% off the cover price. It's quite a bargain! Shipping and handling is just 50¢ per book in the U.S. and 75¢ per book in Canada.* I understand that accepting the 2 free books and gifts places me under no obligation to buy anything. I can always return a shipment and cancel at any time. Even if I never buy another book, the two free books and gifts are mine to keep forever.

194 MDN E4LY 394 MDN E4MC

Name _____ (PLEASE PRINT) _____

Address _____ Apt. # _____

City _____ State/Prov. _____ Zip/Postal Code _____

Signature (if under 18, a parent or guardian must sign)

Mail to **The Reader Service:**
IN U.S.A.: P.O. Box 1867, Buffalo, NY 14240-1867
IN CANADA: P.O. Box 609, Fort Erie, Ontario L2A 5X3

Not valid for current subscribers to the Romance Collection
or the Romance/Suspense Collection.

Want to try two free books from another line?
Call 1-800-873-8635 or visit www.morefreebooks.com.

* Terms and prices subject to change without notice. Prices do not include applicable taxes. N.Y. residents add applicable sales tax. Canadian residents will be charged applicable provincial taxes and GST. Offer not valid in Quebec. This offer is limited to one order per household. All orders subject to approval. Credit or debit balances in a customer's account(s) may be offset by any other outstanding balance owed by or to the customer. Please allow 4 to 6 weeks for delivery. Offer available while quantities last.

Your Privacy: Harlequin Books is committed to protecting your privacy. Our Privacy Policy is available online at www.eHarlequin.com or upon request from the Reader Service. From time to time we make our lists of customers available to reputable third parties who may have a product or service of interest to you. If you would prefer we not share your name and address, please check here. ☐

Help us get it right—We strive for accurate, respectful and relevant communications. To clarify or modify your communication preferences, visit us at www.ReaderService.com/consumerchoice.

MROM10

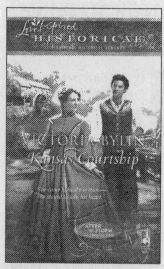

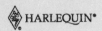
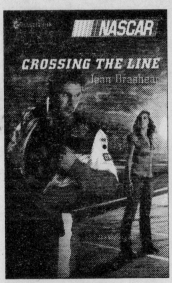